Wife of

The Miller

The Yeoman

The Man of Law

# The Canterbury Tales

## of

# Geoffrey Chaucer

# The Canterbury

# Tales of Geoffrey Chaucer

Selected and Adapted by
## A. Kent Hieatt and Constance Hieatt

Illustrated by
## Gustaf Tenggren

With an Introduction by
## Mark Van Doren

Golden Press  New York

Library of Congress Catalog Card Number: 61-9183

# Contents

# Heere bigynneth the Book of the Tales of Caunterbury

Whan that Aprille with his shoures soote
The droghte of March hath perced to the roote
And bathed every veyne in swich licour
Of which vertu engendred is the flour
Whan Zephirus eek with his sweete breeth
Inspired hath in every holt and heeth
The tendre croppes and the yonge sonne
Hath in the Ram his halve cours yronne
And smale foweles maken melodye
That slepen al the nyght with open ye
So priketh hem nature in hir corages
Thanne longen folk to goon on pilgrimages
And palmeres for to seken straunge strondes
To ferne halwes kowthe in sondry londes
And specially from every shires ende
Of Engelond to Caunterbury they wende
The hooly blisful martir for to seke
That hem hath holpen whan that they were seeke.

# Introduction

**Geoffrey Chaucer**

who died in 1400, was then and still is one of the most lovable of English poets. He is lovable because he is loving, and because he is humorous and real. No poet, no storyteller, is more real than Chaucer, not even Shakespeare; and the reason for this, in so far as any reason can be found, lies in his comic genius.

The sense of humor, rightly considered, is the sense of reality: the sense of what the world is actually like, whether we want it to be or not, and of how human beings think, feel, talk, and behave. Chaucer never goes wrong in this region; he is wise and charitable, like any man who has kept his eyes open and lived well in the world of men. There seems to be nothing that he does not understand as it ought to be understood—

sanely, without false sentiment or unexamined illusion. He knows the place of illusion too, but he keeps it in that place, smiling at the follies and extravagances which he is willing to suggest he shares with the rest of us. There is nobody quite like Chaucer; or, to put it backward, there is no man who is more like other men than he.

He is most famous for his *Canterbury Tales*, a work he did not live to finish, although this fact is unimportant in view of the riches that remain. It is a collection of stories, written in Middle English—the English of his time—and for the most part in verse, of which Chaucer is one of the sweetest masters. The present volume adapts eleven of these stories for young modern readers, and does so in prose—with the amusing exception of "Sir Topas," which

Mr. and Mrs. Hieatt have rendered in a doggerel that corresponds in flavor to that of the original fragment.

Nothing is more characteristic of Chaucer than that he should have said to the Host, as he rode with the rest of the pilgrims to Canterbury: "I just don't know any stories at all." They were all supposed to tell stories, and now Chaucer's turn had come. But he begged off, as Socrates did in Plato's dialogue called *The Symposium*; the topic in *The Symposium* was love, and every man at the banquet was expected to make a speech about it, but Socrates said he had no speech in him; he could only ask a few questions. So Chaucer could only reel off a rime he had learned in his youth. But there was a deeper reason for his refusal, which of course has its funny side when we remember that Chaucer is one of the world's finest storytellers. It was literally true that he had no tale of his own with which to entertain the pilgrims. The tales he told were all retold; he had to find them elsewhere first. He was an adapter, as in their turn the Hieatts are.

When he adapted a story he made it his own by coloring it in accord with his comic genius. Take, for instance, the first and longest story in this book, "The Knight's Tale," which he borrowed from Boccaccio. It deals with courtly lovers—medieval lovers, that is to say, of the sort so common in the literature Chaucer knew that he might have dismissed them as too conventional for serious consideration. And in a sense he does do this. The antics and postures of courtly love—the falling sick at the sight of a beautiful lady, the dedication of one's life to her even though she remained ignorant that she had been seen, the raptures, the despairs, the absolutes of adoration and devotion—could not have seemed real to Chaucer, whose imagination never falsified or exaggerated the truth. Yet he does not so much dismiss

Palamon and Arcite as receive them into his affectionate, smiling mind where all the things that people do, crazy or not, somehow belong. "Meanwhile," says Chaucer at one point, "Palamon remained in the darkness of perpetual imprisonment, and his suffering was doubled by his futile love for Emily. His sorrow was indescribable, and might as well be passed over because some things are too unbearable to talk about."

Now almost any other poet of the time would have thought that Palamon's sorrow *was* describable; indeed, it would be the poet's chief opportunity to rave. But Chaucer never raves; rather, he lets high and great things gently down to ground level where he himself feels most at home. Theseus, duke of Athens, is more his man. Listen to the way he talks about the two lovers. "Look at these two nice young men, Arcite and Palamon. The lady for whom they've been having all this fun and cutting themselves into small pieces doesn't even know them any more than the cuckoo in the air or the hare on the ground! What do you think of that? But people have to try everything, whether it's hot or cold, high or low. A man has to be a fool, whether he's young or old: I know from personal experience." This could be Chaucer talking, as of course it actually is. The voice is the voice of wisdom and forbearance; not of scorn, not of contempt, but rather of ripe, fond understanding of the fools all mortals be.

When Arcite and Palamon were fighting in the grove Chaucer tells us that every blow of their swords "looked as though it would cut down a tree." There is a touch of mockery in the comparison, as there is in the comparison made by the Wife of Bath between her hero, another knight, and—but here are her words: "He married her very privately in the morning, but he was so unhappy to have such an ugly, elderly wife that he hid himself for the rest of the day as if he were an owl."

Who but Chaucer would have written that last word, so surprising, so absurd, and yet so right for his purpose, which was to bring the knight back into the circle of real men? Readers of the book will get a similar pleasure from the image of the mouse and the meat in "The Manciple's Tale"; or—by a reverse process, for in this case the comparison goes up rather than down—from Chaucer's statement in "The Nuns' Priest's Tale" that "Chanticleer sang more merrily than a mermaid." Two things could scarcely be more unlike than a rooster and a mermaid, but again the effect is finally right: the rooster becomes more ridiculous than ever, at the same time that we like him even better than we did before.

Perhaps there is no mockery in Chaucer's treatment of the duke's obsession in the Clerk's tale of Griselda with the idea that he should test his poor wife's loyalty to him. This must have seemed utterly mad to Chaucer, as it does to us; but he lets the duke off with a very mild sentence: "Still, he could not resist the needless desire to test her again and again." The mere fact is so appalling that Chaucer makes no comment on it; he trusts it to comment upon itself; and all the while he is suggesting that it is not too extraordinary for men to act like this. They act strangely at best, and are more to be pitied than censured.

As for women—well, many of the tales provide an opportunity to jest at the expense of wives, and Chaucer lets the jest be made; but he hastens to save himself in "The Nuns' Priest's Tale," after he has pointed out that Chanticleer's misfortune results from his taking the advice of Pertelote, with a sage parenthesis: "Women's advice is all too often bad—it was taking a woman's advice that drove Adam from Paradise. (Or so they say—I don't mean to offend anyone! I certainly have nothing against women!)"

Mr. and Mrs. Hieatt, adapting Chaucer for a special audience, have taken the same kind of liberties with him that he took with the authors he rewrote. Apart from the principal circumstance that they employ prose instead of verse, they abridge, re-arrange, and paraphrase with a gay assurance that their poet would approve. And I think he would. He would recognize in them a solid acquaintance with his entire work, and a deep, fresh sympathy with it, entitling them to present him as they please.

They have pleased to write a rapid, witty, sensible prose which comes as near as prose could come to the effect he was normally after. The stories as they tell them read so easily that in some cases they are finished before the reader has taken a second breath; such a case, notably, is "The Pardoner's Tale," with its swift and terrible climax. Also, if Chaucer were alive now I suspect that he himself might have wanted the name of Chanticleer's song to be "My Love Is Like a Red, Red Rose"; he did not know Burns, so he gave the song another name, popular in his time rather than ours. And I cannot doubt that he would have enjoyed hearing the magician in "The Franklin's Tale" repeat a phrase of Shakespeare: "Our revels now are ended." The magician said in fact: "Al our revel was ago." Which was near enough, but a little learning makes it better.

Our adapters conclude their charming book with some charming advice: "Eat your next good dinner in honor of Geoffrey Chaucer." To this I hope I may add: "And after dinner, read on in *The Canterbury Tales*."

Mark Van Doren

# General Prologue
## of the Canterbury Pilgrims

When the showers of April bathe the earth and nourish a fresh crop of grass and flowers, and when the west wind stirs the new leaves budding on the trees, the birds return to us from their winter homes and make the warm days merry with their music. This is the time, too, when people long to journey to distant shores and to make pilgrimages to faraway holy places in strange lands. And especially, at this time of the year, people from every corner of England journey to Canterbury to visit the

shrine of the martyr Saint Thomas à Becket. When we feel strength renewed in us, as it is in the land itself after the harsh winter, it seems right to give thanks to Saint Thomas, whom we prayed to when we were sick.

It was such a spring when I set out from London to make my pilgrimage to Canterbury. I stopped overnight at an inn called the Tabard, south of the river Thames. That same night twenty-nine more pilgrims stopped at the inn, all bound for Canterbury. It was a good inn, and we were very comfortable and cheerful there. During the evening I got to know these pilgrims, and we all agreed to leave together for Canterbury early in the morning.

The trip from there to Canterbury took four days, and on the way a good many things happened: there was story-telling, but that wasn't all. Some of the pilgrims became great friends, and some quarreled bitterly. Before I tell the stories we told, and what happened on the trip, I think it proper to explain what kind of people these pilgrims were—besides, you'll enjoy the stories more if you know the people who were telling them.

Among the pilgrims there were almost all the kinds of people there are in England. There were men and women, young people and old people, city people and country people, people who had duties in the church and people who made their living by business, professional people, poor people, rich people, good people, and not-so-good people —all brought together by chance, because they were traveling toward Canterbury.

We were honored to have a KNIGHT with us, a nobleman who was a valiant warrior and a true and courteous gentleman. With him was his son, a young SQUIRE, and one servant, a merry YEOMAN clad in green who carried a sheaf of arrows with peacock feathers.

A number of the clergy were in the party, including two nuns, one of whom was a lady PRIORESS, a dainty, well-bred gentlewoman. A NUNS' PRIEST rode with the nuns. There was also a MONK, but not the kind that stays in the cloister and studies— this monk was more likely to be found wherever there was good company, good hunting, and good food. A begging FRIAR was there, too. He didn't look much like a poor scholar or a cloistered monk either, but more like a bishop or a pope in his fine, heavy robe. When he played the harp his eyes twinkled in his head like the stars on a frosty night. We also had with us a CLERK, a poor student at Oxford, who was so thin he looked absolutely hollow—he cared more for books and learning than for fine robes. One other priest was with us, a poor PARSON, who was also a good and learned man. With him rode his brother, a simple and cheerful PLOWMAN.

Two other men were along whose work connected them with the church, but they hardly looked it. One was a SUMMONER, a man whose horrible, fiery red face frightened little children. He was a coarse and ignorant fellow, and when he wasn't out summoning people to appear at court you'd generally find him drinking at a tavern. Beside him rode a PARDONER, who had just come from Rome with a satchelful of pardons that he said were signed by the Pope. He carried with him some worthless things that he said were "relics"—such as a piece of an old pillowcase that he swore was the Virgin Mary's veil—and fooled many simple people into buying them from him at high prices. As we rode along he sang "Come hither, love, to me," in a duet with the Summoner.

Several of our party were distinguished and prosperous men. There was a wealthy MERCHANT, and a PHYSICIAN—a learned Doctor of Medicine who knew the causes and cures of every illness. A MAN OF LAW,

wary and discreet, was also there, who could recite by heart every law in the land. With him rode a FRANKLIN, a well-to-do landowner. The Franklin had often represented his county in Parliament, and was a Justice of the Peace. A group of London tradesmen rode with us, too, and they had brought along their own COOK, one of the best in London, but a bit of a scoundrel, too.

A SHIPMAN, a bold sailor who knew every harbor in Europe, was with us. He was a dangerous customer who liked to make people walk the plank. There was also a good WIFE, a widow from the city of Bath. The Wife of Bath had a bold, fair, red face. She had had many admirers in her youth, as well as five husbands, all of them now dead. She wore a hat as broad as a

shield over the heavy kerchiefs wound around her head, and her stockings were scarlet red.

The other members of the party were a REEVE and a MILLER, a MANCIPLE and myself—there were no more. The Miller was a brawny fellow with a wart on his nose, and with long hairs growing from the wart. The Manciple was quiet, but clever and shrewd in his business dealings. The group of lawyers whom he bought food and drink for, as a kind of purchasing agent, got value for their money—but the Manciple saw to it that he himself made a profit on every deal. The Reeve was thin and had a sour disposition. Like the Manciple, he took such great care of the estate where he was overseer that his lord was well satisfied— but the Reeve always ended up with a tidy profit for himself.

All these pilgrims were gathered at the Tabard Inn that night, and I was one of them. While we sat at supper, our HOST—a man named Harry Bailey who owned the inn—happened to think of a good idea for amusing us while we would be riding all that weary way. The host himself had already impressed us by his friendliness and talkativeness. He was a companionable, large, handsome man who liked nothing better than merrymaking. So as we were together that night he said to us, "I haven't seen a merrier band of pilgrims all year, even though they all come by here on their way to Canterbury. I know that on the way you'll be telling jokes and stories, because there's no point in just riding along as though you were so many deaf-mutes. You might as well be bags of wheat on horseback unless you can get a little fun out of the trip. But why don't you get things organized? My proposition is this: Suppose each one of you tells two stories on the way to Canterbury and two on the way back.

What's more, if you promise to do this, I'll go all the way with you and be your guide as well as the manager of the story-telling. Then, when we get back here, whoever has told the best tale can have a free supper, paid for by all the rest of the company. What do you say?"

We all agreed that this was a fine idea, although it occurred to some of us that Harry Bailey was a shrewd businessman who stood to make some profit from serving us that supper. But we knew he was good-hearted, and, besides, he had already served us a fine meal, with excellent wine, so we all promised that we would carry out our parts in the plan. We had more wine to con-firm the agreement before we went to bed.

In the morning, when day began to break, our Host gathered us all together and we rode off on the road to Canterbury. When we had gone a short distance, our Host stopped and said, "Now, my lords, remember our agreement—let's see who shall tell the first tale. You've all agreed that I am to be judge and have the final word in all disputes. Anyone who rebels against my judgment must pay for every-thing we spend along the way. Now draw lots before we go any further: the one who gets the short straw must begin. Sir Knight, my master and my lord, draw your cut. Come near, my lady Prioress, and you, sir Clerk—don't be bashful! Everyone draw his lot."

We all drew right away, and it happened —whether by chance or the Host's plan— that the lot fell to the Knight. Everyone was pleased with this, since the Knight's modest appearance made us sure that he was a good man, besides being a brave one. Although he had won honors in war all over the world, fighting for his faith, he was plainly dressed in a coarse tunic stained with rusty marks from his coat of mail. He had just come back from a campaign.

The good Knight did not hesitate to keep his word. He said "Since I must begin the game, so be it! Let us ride on."

With that we rode on, and the Knight began cheerfully to tell a tale, as you will hear. The story was a very long one— longer than any of the others after it—and it was about love and a great tournament fought for love's sake.

# THE KNIGHT'S TALE
## Palamon and Arcite

The ancient stories tell us that there was once a duke of Athens named Theseus, who was the noblest conqueror under the sun. With his wisdom and his prowess he won many rich countries for his own. He even went as far as the distant country of Scythia, which was ruled by a race of warlike women called Amazons. He conquered them, too, and won the love of their queen, the valiant and gracious Hippolita. He mar-

ried her, and conveyed her home toward Athens along with her younger sister, the radiant Emily.

Theseus rode home surrounded by a great host of conquering warriors. Just outside Athens he suddenly came upon a company quite different from his own. Before him in the road, kneeling two by two, was a column of noble ladies, weeping and lamenting. They were all dressed in black, and

they would not stop their mournful outcry until he had come up to them, and the first of them had caught the reins of his horse in her hands.

"What people are you?" asked Theseus. "Why are you disturbing the festival of my triumphal return? Are you dejected because of my good fortune and honor, or is it that someone has harmed you in some way? Tell me whether any wrong that has been done to you can be righted, and tell me, too, why it is that you all wear black."

The eldest of the ladies nearly collapsed for sorrow but at last brought herself to speak. "Indeed, Lord Theseus, we are not grieved by your glory and honor. You have had the good fortune to gain a great victory, but we have had the evil fortune to lose what is most precious of all to us. Instead of envying you your great conquest, we ask only that you share in our great grief and take pity on us. There is not one of us, my lord, who has not been a duchess or a queen, but now we are all brought to misery, for that is the way of worldly fortune. It works like a great cartwheel: you may sit on its upper edge, but suddenly the wheel turns, and you are down in the mire. We have been waiting for you beside this road for two weeks.

"I who am weeping and wailing before you was once the wife of King Capaneus, who died at the siege of the city of Thebes, alas the day! And all the others that you see here, lamenting in their black attire—all of us lost our husbands in that bloody battle. A man named Creon has won the victory and has become the tyrant-ruler of Thebes, but he has so little pity on our misfortune that he will not allow the dead bodies of our husbands to be buried or to be burned, as is our custom. The villain has simply piled them in a heap and released dogs upon them to dishonor them." And with that, all the

women fell groveling on their faces and cried out, "Have mercy, lord, upon us wretched women!"

The heart of the gentle duke Theseus was filled with pity. He swore an oath as a true knight to do everything in his power to avenge them so fiercely that all Greece should speak of how Creon's guilt was punished by Theseus. Then, without a moment's delay, he turned around and prepared to ride with his army to Thebes.

In spite of the campaign he had just fought, Theseus was so enraged at the injustice of Creon that he would not rest for even half a day. He sent Hippolita and Emily into Athens and marched away with his noble army. His great white banner bearing the red figure of Mars, the god of

slain in the battle. Among others they found, lying side by side, two young knights who had been sorely wounded but who would probably recover. Their rich suits of armor were exactly alike, and Theseus' heralds, who knew about such things, recognized them as two important enemies whom Theseus could not allow to escape. Their names were Arcite and Palamon; their mothers were sisters, and—most important of all—these knights were of the royal blood of Thebes. If they escaped to fight another day, they would be likely to cause the noble duke trouble. Consequently, when servants had gently carried the two young men before Theseus in his tent, he sent them off to be imprisoned forever in his city of Athens. They could not even be ransomed with great sums of gold, in the way that knights usually are when they are captured, for they were too dangerous ever to be freed.

In a few days, then, the situation seemed to be settled. Theseus rode home to Athens crowned with laurel as a conqueror, and there he lived in joy and honor. Palamon and Arcite, however, were imprisoned in a tower, to live in anguish and woe even after they had recovered from their wounds.

So things continued, day after day, and year after year, until one fine May morning Hippolita's sister Emily rose early to stroll in the castle garden. Emily herself was fairer than the lily on its green stalk, and fresher than the newest flowers of May. It cannot be said which was more beautiful —the colors of roses or the glowing tint of her face. She had put on fresh clothes, and her golden hair was in a braid almost a yard long down her back. As the sun rose, she was walking up and down in the garden, gathering fresh, spring flowers to twine into a garland for her head, and singing like an angel in heaven.

war, glittered before him. His pennon of gold was richly embroidered with the image of the Minotaur, the enormous beast that Theseus had killed in Crete long before, and his army was the flower of all knighthood as he bore down upon Creon.

The battle at Thebes was short. Theseus defeated the army of Creon with great slaughter and slew Creon himself in personal combat. Then, like a true and gentle knight, he restored to all the sorrowing ladies the remains of their noble husbands. He saw to it that their bodies were suitably consumed by fire on a funeral pyre, according to the custom of the ancient Greeks. Then he bade the ladies a gentle farewell.

Meanwhile Theseus' men hunted through the piles of Creon's warriors who had been

The great, sullen tower in which Palamon and Arcite were imprisoned was right next to the garden. Palamon and Arcite paced its uppermost chamber, as their jailer by habit allowed them to do, for from there they could see all the noble city, as well as the leafy garden. As usual, Palamon was bewailing his sad case to himself, but by chance or fate he happened to look out through the iron grille of the window and see fair Emily as she wandered about. He turned quite pale and cried aloud.

Arcite heard Palamon's cry and jumped up to comfort him, thinking that his cousin was mourning their sad lot. "My dear cousin," he said, "why do you look so pale, as though you were a corpse? Why do you cry out? There is nothing here that could hurt you, except the prison itself, and that we shall have to endure patiently. Neither we nor any other man can resist the workings of fortune's wheel. What can we do?"

"You are mistaken, dear cousin," answered Palamon. "What caused me to cry out this time was not the prison, but a vision that has entered my eyes and lodged in my heart. The fairness of that lady yonder in the garden is the cause of my sorrow. Her beauty is such that I do not know whether she is really a woman or the very goddess of love." And so saying, he fell down on his knees as though he actually would pray to a goddess, and uttered these words: "Venus, if it was by your will that you are now appearing before my eyes, hear my prayer. Help us to escape from this prison, or if captivity is our eternal destiny, at least give aid to our noble family that has fallen so low through the workings of tyranny."

Arcite was amazed. He, too, gazed out the window and beheld Emily walking to and fro. But, just as with Palamon, the sight of her beauty wounded him to the heart, and he sighed. "The fresh beauty of the lady has brought me near my death. If I may not have her mercy and her grace, so that I can at least be with her, I shall die; there is no other remedy."

Palamon, who had been his friend for so long, glowered at these words. Grimly he said, "Are you joking or in earnest?"

"In earnest, by my faith," answered Arcite. "So help me, joking is the farthest thing from my mind."

Palamon scowled. "It would be no great honor to you," he said, "to be false to one with whom you have sworn the strongest oath of brotherhood. You remember your oath, and mine—you can't deny that. Each of us swore never to hinder the other in love, or in anything else, until death should part us, even if we were submitted to the cruelest tortures. You swore, furthermore, to aid me faithfully in every undertaking, and I swore the same to you. Yet now you dare to love the lady whom I love and serve, and ever shall. False Arcite, you shall not have your wish! I loved her first and told my sorrow to you. You are bound on your honor as a knight to help me if you can. If you do not, you are false!"

Arcite answered him pridefully and wrathfully, "You would be false more readily than I. And false you are! I was the first to love her as a knight should love a lady—not you. How can you deny it? You don't know whether she's a woman or a goddess! You feel nothing but a religious adoration for her; I love her as a woman and a human being, and what has just happened to me I told you as my sworn brother. Even if I supposed you did love her first, don't you know the proverb? 'Love knows no law!' If a man is in love, he simply can't help it.

"You know that people break all kinds of laws daily for the sake of love. Besides, when you come down to it, you aren't ever likely to gain her, and neither am I. You know yourself that you and I are condemned to prison for life. We're like the two dogs that fought all day for a bone: a vulture swooped down and got the bone while they were snarling at each other. In love it's each man for himself. Love her, if you want to. I'll go on loving her always, no matter what you do. Each of us will simply have to endure his lot forever in this prison."

But that didn't settle their argument. It went on and on, becoming more and more furious as time passed.

It happened one day that a duke named Pirithous came to visit Theseus. The two men were as good friends as Palamon and Arcite had once been, and they had undertaken many valiant enterprises together. They were so devoted to each other that neither of them could deny the other anything he wanted. By chance, Pirithous was also a good friend of Arcite, whom he had known well at Thebes, and he asked Theseus to release the young knight. Theseus could not deny his good friend's request, and Arcite was finally released. Palamon was left in prison.

Theseus knew the danger of releasing so important an enemy, and forced Arcite to promise that he would never more appear, even for an hour, in any part of Theseus' country. If he did, he would lose his head. So as soon as the young knight was released, he left at once for Thebes.

Arcite was even sadder there than he had been in Athens. He said to himself, "This is a worse prison than the one I was in before! I wish that I had never known Pirithous because now I can never see Emily again. If I could only see her from my prison window, that would be enough. Perhaps Palamon, who is still there, will be able to do even more than see her. He is a worthy knight, and perhaps he can get into her good graces, but I have no chance for anything of the sort." He wept and wailed, and even thought of ending his life.

But Palamon, back in his prison, thought that he was even worse off than Arcite. "Arcite is free and a good knight," he wailed to himself. "Perhaps he will gather an army and attack Theseus, and then it may happen that he will win Emily. Here I can do nothing, but he has complete freedom of action." And jealousy gnawed at his heart until he could hardly endure his fate.

Who knows which of these young men had the harder time of it? Palamon was condemned to remain in prison until he died, but he could see Emily occasionally from his window; Arcite was exiled from Athens forever, upon pain of losing his head, so that he could never see Emily.

Arcite was so sorrowful that he could neither eat nor sleep. He grew thin; his eyes sank into his head; his face grew pale. He wouldn't talk to anyone, and if he heard music he wept, thinking about Emily. After a year or two he even started seeing visions.

One night it seemed to him that Mercury, the messenger of the gods, came to him and told him to go back to Athens, for there he would find a way to end his woe. As soon as he woke from his dream, he decided that this was what he would do, even if it meant having his head cut off. He might as well die seeing Emily, rather than drag out his life in Thebes. He picked up a mirror, looked at himself, and was astonished and overjoyed to see how much he had changed. He suddenly realized that he might go to Athens in disguise without anyone's recognizing him. Therefore, he dressed as a poor laborer, and traveled to Athens.

When he got there, he asked for work with one of the attendants of Emily. He was young and strong, so he could easily drudge at the most menial labor. For a time he worked as a page to Emily, calling himself Philostratus, but he was so gentle and good that the whole court began saying he should

be raised to a higher degree. He had made a strong impression on everyone, and on Theseus in particular, who made him a squire and gave him gold to maintain himself in this new position. He had, besides, the income from his estate in Thebes brought to him secretly. He behaved so discreetly that no one became suspicious about where he got his wealth. In a short time he so won the favor of Theseus that he became his chief squire.

Meanwhile, his sworn brother Palamon remained in the darkness of perpetual imprisonment, and his suffering was doubled by his futile love for Emily. His sorrow was indescribable, and might as well be passed over because some things are too unbearable to talk about. But it happened one May night, seven years after he had first been condemned to prison, that with the help of a friend he arranged to escape. He gave his jailer a drink of wine and honey in which

came by chance to the grove where Palamon was hidden. He jumped down from his charger and wandered up and down on the wooded paths.

Hiding in a thicket, Palamon saw his cousin but did not recognize him. He kept still as death, for he knew that if he were discovered, he would probably lose his life. Arcite on the other hand, had no idea that anyone was watching him: he finished his song and then, like a moody lover, fell suddenly into a melancholy humor and started talking to himself.

"Alas," he sighed, "how long will Thebes remain miserable? I am of the royal family of that great city, and my family is degraded in me to the point where I serve Theseus, my mortal enemy, as his squire. The gods have done me even greater shame, for I cannot even be known by my own name, but must call myself Philostratus. Except for wretched Palamon and me, the whole royal family has been destroyed, and, worst of all, the god of love is bound to kill me with the fiery dart of love that has pierced my heart. Ah, Emily, the bright beams of your eyes are the darts by which I die. The ruin of the royal house of Thebes, and all my other sorrows, would be a trifle if I could only obtain your grace and mercy!" And he almost collapsed thinking of her beauty and her remoteness, for he had never been able to speak to her of his love.

Palamon heard every word, and the cold sword of jealousy sank into his heart as he realized that this man was his sworn brother and at the same time his enemy. He trembled in wrath, and his face turned deadly pale as he sprang from the thicket and addressed Arcite like a madman. "Now I've caught you, false, traitorous Arcite! I know you for what you are: you love my lady, even though you are of my blood and sworn to aid me in all things. I know that you have

he had mixed opium, so that the man slept very soundly and was not disturbed by anything Palamon did.

Late in the night Palamon broke out of the tower and fled Athens in great fear. Since he had only reached the outskirts of the town by morning, he had to hide in a grove of trees. He had formed a plan to wait there all day, and then to go on to Thebes, where he would raise an army with the help of his friends and return to attack Theseus. He had made up his mind to win Emily in this way or lose his life.

That same morning, Arcite, the chief squire of Theseus, had heard the song of the lark and had risen early to see the lusty sun drying the silver dewdrops on the leaves. He thought that he would ride forth outside the town. So he went, on a fiery charger, with nothing on his mind except to weave a garland of woodbine or hawthorn. As Arcite rode along, singing to himself, he

deceived Duke Theseus and changed your name. Now, either you or I shall die! You shall not love my Emily, for I shall be the only one to love her. I am Palamon, your mortal foe, and though I have no weapon, having just escaped from prison, I am certain that you shall stop loving Emily or die on the spot."

When Arcite recognized Palamon, and heard what he had to say, he answered just as wrathfully, pridefully, and bitterly. "By the powers above," he exclaimed, pulling out his sword, "if you were not sick and mad for love, and if you had a sword, you would not pass from this grove without dying by my hand! I defy the oath that you say I have made to you. You fool, love is free, and I'll love her in spite of you. I'd kill you now but for one thing. I know you are a worthy knight and want to reach a decision by knightly combat. I swear that I shall

not fail you tomorrow. I shall bring you the best armor, and take the worst for myself. Furthermore, tonight I'll bring you meat and drink and bedding. And if it be that you kill me tomorrow in this wood, you may have my lady."

Palamon agreed, and they parted, to meet on the following morning according to their knightly word.

Now Cupid, the pitiless god of love, bore down on these two young men as hard as ever the tyrant Creon oppressed the ladies of Thebes. Neither love nor lords will permit any but themselves to rule, and Arcite and Palamon, in great bitterness, carried out their plan under the cruel mastery of Cupid and his law.

The next morning, before sunup, Arcite brought two sets of armor to the grove in utter secrecy. As soon as he and Palamon caught sight of each other, their passion

made them grow pale, like hunters catching sight of a fierce and dangerous bear. Each of them thought to himself, "Here comes my deadly enemy! If I don't kill him, he'll kill me!" Without exchanging a word, Palamon and Arcite armed each other and gripping their spears, fell to thrusting at each other as fiercely as if one were a lion and the other a tiger. They rushed together as wild boars do when they are so murderously angry that their mouths foam white. The blood poured out in streams on the ground around them.

There is no telling what would have happened if they had not been interrupted. But whatever causes it—whatever power watches over us—Theseus happened to be hunting the great stags in the woods that morning, as he did every morning in May. Like a proper lord, he liked nothing better than to spring from his bed before daybreak and ride out royally with hunt and hounds and horn to chase a stag. On this morning he had with him his fair queen Hippolita and her lovely sister Emily, all of them dressed in green. Someone had told him that there was a stag in a nearby grove, so he spurred toward it and stopped a little ways off.

Theseus shielded his eyes with his hand and gazed into the grove, over which the sun was just rising. But what he saw there was no stag—only Arcite and Palamon fighting, by this time with swords that flashed so hideously in the morning sunlight that every blow looked as though it would cut down a tree.

As a lord and ruler who must maintain the peace in his land, Theseus did not hesitate. In a towering rage he spurred his charger between the two men, pulled out his sword fiercely, and cried, "Hold, on pain of losing your heads! By Mars, I'll kill

the man who strikes the next stroke!"
When the two young men had stopped—as
they had to—he went on. "What sort of
men are you, who dare to fight here? Anyone would think you had my permission to
undertake personal combat and joust before
me and my duly appointed judges and
officers."

Palamon and Arcite were in despair at
this turn of events, but Palamon answered
hastily, before Arcite could open his mouth:
"Sire, what good would it do to make ex-
cuses. All is lost. We both deserve to die.
We are two miserable wretches whose very
lives are a trouble to us. As you are a right-
eous lord and judge, give us no mercy, but
slay me first, for holy charity! But kill my
companion as well! Or kill him first! You do
not know it, but this is your deadly foe
Arcite, who was banished from your land
on peril of losing his head. He came back
and said he was Philostratus. He has deceived you for many a year. He has done all
this because he is in love with Emily.

"As for me, since it seems I must die, I
confess that I am that woeful Palamon who
broke out of your prison. I am your mortal
foe, and I love Emily so ardently that I wish
to die in her sight. Therefore I ask that you
give me what I deserve, which is death. But
be sure to kill Arcite too. We both deserve
to be slain."

The worthy duke answered roundly,
"This matter is shortly concluded. You have
condemned yourself by your own statement.
Nothing more is needed. You shall be dead,
by mighty Mars the red!"

But the queen and Emily and their attend-
ant ladies were moved to pity at the thought
of such noble men wounding each other horribly, all for love, and then dying like trai-
tors. They began to weep. They knelt before Theseus, crying out, "Have mercy,
lord, for the sake of us women," just as the

noble ladies had knelt before Theseus in the
road, years before. And Theseus, though he
shook with wrath at what had happened,
gradually calmed himself, for he was a
gentle-hearted man.

With great effort he regained his self-
control and thought to himself, "How can I
blame these knights? When a man's in love,
he will naturally do anything to gain his
lady, and when a man's in prison, he will

do anything to get out." Besides, he had compassion on the weeping women kneeling before him and he softly said to himself, "What good is a lord that will never have mercy on anyone? One kind of person is humble and repentant for what he has done, and another may be prideful and unwilling to leave off his evil deeds. The lord who can't see the difference between these two is just another Creon."

After he had thought his way through to a just decision, he was happy again and started to joke with all those that were around him.

"Look at these two nice young men, Arcite and Palamon. The lady for whom they've been having all this fun and cutting themselves into small pieces doesn't even know them, any more than the cuckoo in the air or the hare on the ground! What do you think of that? But people have to try everything, whether it's hot or cold, high or low. A man has to be a fool, whether he's young or old: I know from personal experience. Having all this in mind, I now render my judgment: Since I know the pain of love, and how it can constrain a man, I hereby forgive completely what you have done, at the request of my queen who kneels here, and of Emily, our dear sister. As for your part of the agreement, you must swear to me that you'll never more harm my country, nor make war upon me, but be my friends in all the ways you can. In a word, you are pardoned."

Then Palamon and Arcite took the oath he wished, and asked him fairly to be their lord and to give them mercy in the matter of Emily, to which he further replied, "Either of you is certainly worthy to marry her, no matter how high her rank; but nevertheless I must speak in the interest of Emily, over whom you have been jealous and vengeful for so long. You know as well as I that she can't marry both of you, even if you go on cutting each other up from here to eternity. One of you is just going to have to go whistle in an ivy leaf.

"I have thought of a way to find out who is destined to have her. Each of you shall go wherever he wants, without ransom and without being under my control. One year from now each shall bring one hundred knights here, armed for a tourney and ready to decide the issue by battle. Then I promise you upon my faith as a knight, I shall give Emily to whichever one of you has the good fortune to win. I shall arrange a suitable place for the tourney, and as I hope mercy for my soul, I shall be a fair and faithful judge of the fighting. If you think this is a good plan, then agree to it here and now, for this is my final decision in your affair."

Palamon's expression changed from sorrow to delight at so just and gracious an offer from their former enemy, and Arcite jumped up for joy. All those present went down on their knees to thank their lord for his generosity. Palamon and Arcite, each hopeful of winning the battle, took their leave and journeyed toward the ancient, broad walls of their city of Thebes.

Duke Theseus immediately built a magnificent amphitheatre, at great expense, for the tourney between the two companies of knights. He made it in an exact circle, a mile wide, with walls of stone sixty yards high; the rows of seats along the inside of the wall were built like a flight of steps: Each row of seats was a little higher than the one in front of it, so that everyone could see comfortably. Huge marble gates were built in the walls on the east and west sides. The whole structure was the most marvelous of its kind in the world, for Theseus hired every skillful architect, painter, and sculptor in the land to make his amphitheatre impressive and beautiful.

For the worship of the gods he built three temples, one above the east gate, another above the western one, and a third in a turret of the north wall. The first was devoted to Venus, the goddess of love; the second to Mars, the god of war; and the third to Diana, the goddess of young girls who are not married. The first temple contained a statue of Venus floating in the green sea, and all around the walls were painted the

beauties and the sorrows of love. The second temple contained a statue of fierce Mars in a chariot, and all around the walls were grisly paintings of his power in battle, in anger, and in violent death. The third temple contained a statue of Diana clothed in green and sitting on the back of a deer, for she is a goddess of hunting as well as of maidens.

Meanwhile Palamon and Arcite had been gathering together their companies of knights, the finest they could find. Many

people thought that there had never in the history of the world been such a company of worthy warriors, for every one of them was a first-class fighter. Palamon and Arcite had no trouble bringing them together, however, because every man who loved knighthood and fame wanted to be one of the company. There were all kinds of mighty warriors among them. Some of them were armed in chain mail; others wore armor of steel plate. Some of them had large shields; others took care to protect their legs with elaborate armor. Some carried battle-axes; others preferred maces with spiked metal heads to crush armor and man.

One of the greatest warriors with Palamon was Lycurgus, king of Thrace. He arrived sitting in a chariot of gold drawn by four white bulls, and around the chariot ran twenty white wolfhounds, each about as large as a steer and each wearing a golden muzzle. He himself had a raven-black beard and black hair hanging down his back, and on his hair was set a wreath of gold, as thick as your arm and set with rubies and dia-monds. The black hairs of his eyebrows fairly bristled as he looked around fiercely. To cover his armor he wore a coal-black bear's skin. A hundred stout lords rode in his company.

With Arcite was the great Emetreus, king of India. He sat upon a great bay steed whose steel trappings were covered with patterned cloth of gold. A rich cloth embroidered with large pearls hung down over his armor in front and back. His saddle was of burnished gold, and a short mantle covered with rubies hung from his shoulder. His hair was yellow and curly, and on it he wore a wreath of green laurel. An eagle rode upon his outstretched arm, and tame lions and leopards ran about his procession, in which there were a hundred lords, in full armor except for their helmets—they wore none while they were in procession so that they might see and be seen more easily.

All the knights of the two companies, and all their followers, arrived one morning in Theseus' city. He housed them nobly and feasted them sumptuously. The minstrels played, the courses of the feast were served magnificently, and everyone received splendid gifts. There was a tremendous stir and activity about the whole town and especially about Theseus' palace, from the hawks sitting on the perch above to the hounds lying on the floor below. The ladies at the feast danced and sang, and the men spoke feelingly of love's joys and sorrows.

But the bustle that went on in public was unimportant compared to the private actions of the two lovers and of Emily, each of whom decided to pray before the battle to the god or goddess that he or she favored.

First Palamon went forth before day-break to the temple of Venus over the east gate of the amphitheatre. Humbly he im-plored her, "Holy lady, yield to me Emily, whom I love so distractedly that I cannot express my pains to you. I promise to be your servant forever if I may possess her. But if you, with your great power in earth and heaven, will not give her to me, then let Arcite send a spear through my heart in the battle; if I am once dead, I shall not care if he wins her for his wife. Blissful lady, this is my prayer."

Then Palamon sacrificed to the goddess, and after a little while her statue shook and made a sign that seemed to him to mean that his prayer would be granted. The time it took the statue to respond seemed to show that there would be some delay, but Palamon was well satisfied and went back to his lodging with a happy heart.

Shortly after this, at sunrise, Emily got up and went with her maidens to the temple of Diana on the north side of the amphi-theatre. They took along the incense, the clothing, and the honey-wine in drinking horns that were suitable for a sacrifice to this goddess. Emily's golden hair hung down her back, and on her head she wore an ever-green wreath. She lighted two fires upon Diana's altar and made her prayer in these words: "Maiden goddess of the greenwood, you well know that I desire to remain ever in your service and never to marry. Like you, I love to roam the woods and hunt. I pray that by your great power you may restore peace and friendship between Pala-mon and Arcite. Turn their hearts away from me and quench their passion. But if it be that you will not grant me this boon and that it is my fate to marry one of them, then send me the one that loves me best. Behold my bitter tears, and preserve me from the harm of love."

The two fires were burning brightly on the altar as Emily prayed, but suddenly one fire went out completely and then started burning again. After that, the other fire went out completely, and as it went out, it gave off a hissing sound, as burning wood does when it is wet. From the ends of the smoldering sticks drops of blood ran out. Emily was terrified. She did not know what these strange happenings meant, but they seemed so unnatural and threatening to her that she started to weep.

At that point the goddess Diana herself appeared before her. She carried her bow in hand and was dressed as a huntress. She said to the panic-stricken girl, "Daughter, you must bring your sorrowing to an end. The gods have decreed by their eternal word that you shall marry one of those young men who have suffered so much for you, but I may not tell you which one it is. The two fires that were burning on my altar here have made a sign that shows what will happen to your two lovers." With that Diana strode forth, so that the arrows rattled in her quiver as she moved; then she disappeared into thin air. Emily went home, wondering what the two fires had to do with Palamon and Arcite.

Shortly after this, Arcite went to the temple of Mars over the west gate of the amphitheatre. He prayed in the following words: "O mighty god of war, accept my poor sacrifice and yield me my heart's desire. I am young and inexperienced, as you know, and I am more maddened by love than anyone ever was. My lady does not care what happens to me, and I cannot marry her unless I win the tournament.

Therefore, fierce lord, help me to gain the victory in the fight. If you will grant my request, I shall always serve you by carrying on wars. I shall cut off my beard and hair, which have never yet felt the razor, and I shall offer them up to you. Give me the victory. This is all I ask."

As Arcite ended his prayer, the great doors of the temple began to rattle and clash without anyone's touching them. The fire

burned more strongly on the altar, so that the whole temple was brightly lit. The sweet smell of incense rose from the floor. Arcite was somewhat frightened, but he raised his hand and threw more incense on the fire. Then the armor on the statue of Mars rattled, and Arcite heard the low, dull murmur of a voice which seemed to utter indistinctly the single word "Victory!" He was sure that he had gained his request, and went happily back to his lodging.

But in the heavens, where the gods live, there arose a great argument, for Venus had promised Palamon that he should have Emily, and Mars had promised Arcite victory in the battle that was to be fought for her hand. Venus wept, and Mars stormed, until there seemed no end to their argument, although Jupiter, king of the gods, tried to quiet them. Finally old Saturn, the grandfather of the immortal gods, used the knowledge that he had gained from his long life to find a way out of their difficulties. "Dear daughter Venus," he said, "it is not usually my way to settle arguments, because I generally like to encourage them. But since I am your grandfather, and Mars', I shall use my great power to end your dispute. Dry your tears, for I shall see to it that your knight Palamon will have his lady, although Arcite, the knight of Mars, shall have the victory. You will see how I shall arrange it."

The same day that Palamon, Emily, and Arcite had made their prayers, all of those who had come to fight and all the court of Theseus passed their time in jousting and dancing. Everyone was happy because of the great festival and because it was again the month of May. But in spite of the festivity, they all went to bed early to be ready for the great tourney the next day.

On that day there was more bustle than before, because all the last-minute prepara-

tions had to be made for the fighting. There was whinnying of horses and rattling of harness in all the lodgings. Groups of lords were seen riding to the palace, and everywhere you could see harness and armor with the richest and strangest designs that could be made in gold, in embroidery, and in steel. The highly-colored shields glittered in the sun. The horses had on their decorated head-armor and their low-hanging trappings. Coats of mail, helmets inlaid with gold, and the colorful embroidered coverings worn over each knight's armor were seen in every direction. Squires were busily fastening the steel heads on the spears, buckling the helmets, and fitting armstraps to the shields. Impatient horses with foaming mouths gnawed restlessly on their golden bridles and pranced. Armorers spurred from this place to that with their files and hammers, and yeomen eagerly gathered on foot along with the commoners, who carried short, thick staffs. Pipes, trumpets, and kettledrums were readied to make their fierce noise in battle.

The palace was full of people going up and down. Here three of them would gather in a group, and there ten, all gossiping about who was the strongest fighter. Some were sure that it would go one way; others were just as sure that it would go the other. One man said, "That one really looks grim; he's sure to fight hard." Another man said, "This one has a battle-axe that weighs twenty pounds; you can bet on him." Everyone tried to act like an expert and impress his neighbors.

Duke Theseus was awakened early in the morning by all the hubbub, but he stayed in his chamber until Palamon and Arcite were brought to the palace. Then he mounted a throne in a window that looked out on the crowd, and all the people pressed forward to honor their mighty duke, and hear what he had to say. His herald mounted a platform below and called out until all the noise had stopped; then he proclaimed the wishes of Theseus.

"Our noble lord," said the herald, "has decided in his great wisdom that it would be foolish to carry this battle to the death. Therefore he decrees that no one bring into the place of tourney any dart or arrow, or any battle-axe or any dagger or short sword to stab with. The knights may ride at each other only once with spears, although they may thrust with them on foot to defend themselves. After that they may fight only with long swords and maces. Furthermore a wooden post will be put up for each company, and whoever is captured shall be brought to the post on the other company's side, where he must stay, without fighting, until the end of the tourney. And if either Palamon or Arcite is captured or killed, then the battle will be over and no one may continue fighting. Now may God speed you: go forth, and fight hard! This is our lord's will."

All the people cried out so that the noise went far up into the sky, "God save our lord, who is so good that he wishes no one to die!" The trumpets suddenly blared forth, and the whole company rode forth to the amphitheatre. They went through the city, where the buildings along the street were hung with cloth of gold. Theseus rode first, with Palamon and Arcite on either side. After them came the queen and Emily, and then the others, two by two, according to their rank. By the middle of the morning they had reached the amphitheatre and Theseus was seated on his royal chair, with the queen and Emily and their ladies ranged around him. All the people pressed in and took their seats.

Suddenly, Arcite entered with his hundred knights through the west gate under the temple of Mars. They bore a red banner. At the same moment Palamon rode in at the east gate, under the temple of Venus, with his hundred knights bearing a white banner. Each company ranged itself in a single line, and their names were called out to make sure that each leader had exactly a hundred knights. Then the gates were shut, and a herald cried out, "Now do your duty, young knights!" The attendants stopped their busy riding up and down. The trumpets blew.

Silently, every knight in the two opposing lines lowered his spear, couched it in the shoulder socket of his armor, and braced for the attack. In went the spurs into the horses' sides, and the two lines rushed together. Then it was every man for himself. Spears broke against shields or pierced through the armor so that a knight would shudder with the deadly thrust; or spears bent against

shield or armor and then sprang up from knights' hands twenty feet into the air, falling back end over end in the sunlight. When the charge was over, out came the swords from their scabbards and shimmered as they were flourished to and fro.

Swords hewed helmets to pieces and the blood burst out in sudden red streams. The spiked heads of the maces came down hard again and again, crushing armor and bones. One knight thrust through the thickest of the throng; another one's steed stumbled, and down went horse and man. Here a man thrown from his horse would roll like a ball through the hurly-burly of the fight; there another dismounted knight would thrust for his life with the shaft of his spear. Here a knight would gallop such a course that with his spear he hurled down another knight and his horse both, and they fell with a crash. Another knight was badly wounded and then captured; he was led to the post on the other side, in spite of all he could do, and then there was no help for it: he could fight no more that day. Another knight was captured and led away to the other side. The fight went on hour after hour, with pauses as Theseus proclaimed them to rest the fighters.

Palamon and Arcite fought like wild beasts. They often met during the course of the fight and wounded each other grievously. They fought with many others as well, and each of the heroes unhorsed two knights apiece. Just before the sun went down they were fighting together again. Their swords bit through each other's helmets so that the blood ran down their sides, and their wild jealousy made each of them bitterly wish to end the other's life. Suddenly Arcite's

friend King Emetreus came at Palamon from the side and gave him a deep sword-wound; with that, twenty other knights caught him and pulled him toward their post. His knights did their best to rescue him, but in vain. King Lycurgus was knocked off his horse, and Palamon was gradually dragged away, although before he was taken he struck Emetreus hard enough to throw him a sword's length out of his saddle. When they got him with a great effort to the post, there was nothing he could do. No matter how desperate he was, he had to stop fighting.

As soon as Theseus saw that Palamon had been captured, he cried out, "Ho! No more fighting! The tourney is finished. As an honest judge I proclaim that Arcite of Thebes shall have Emily, for by his good fortune he has won her fairly." Everyone shouted so loud that it seemed the amphitheatre would fall in. In the heavens Venus could now do nothing for her knight. "I am put to shame," she said, and she wept so hard that her tears fell like rain into the field. But Saturn reassured her, saying, "Daughter, hold your peace. Mars has his will now. His knight has won what he asked for, but by my head, your turn will come soon."

The trumpets blew and the heralds shouted. Arcite took off his helmet and rode his horse along the stands, looking up at Emily. She cast a shy look down at him, for she knew he had won her. But at this moment, when Arcite had achieved his heart's desire, Saturn's plan went into effect. A grisly ghost sent from the infernal regions suddenly started up from the ground before Arcite's horse. Terrified, the horse turned abruptly and reared at the same time, so that he lost his footing and fell forward. Arcite was pitched out of his saddle toward the horse's head, and, with

his feet still in the stirrups, he swung down so his chest struck against a steel knob on the front of his saddle. He fell flat on the ground. His attendants and friends picked him up and bore him to the palace. Then they cut his armor off him and put him to bed as quickly as they could. He was still conscious, and calling out for Emily.

Theseus did not want to discomfort the whole company on account of this misfortune, so he rode back to his palace with pomp and ceremony, as though nothing had happened. The doctors had told him that Arcite would probably not die, so no one needed to be unhappy. Besides, everyone was glad that no one had been killed, although many of the knights were badly wounded. They put salves on all the wounds and on the broken bones, and they repeated charms that were supposed to cure anyone hurt in battle. All the wounded knights also

drank medicines made of herbs to save their arms and legs. Theseus gave them an all-night banquet, and fortunately they could not argue with each other jealously about who had been cowardly and who not. They had all done well.

No one thought there was any discredit in being unhorsed, because it could happen to anyone; and the knights who had been captured and forced to the stake all received due credit, because they had been overcome by superior numbers, as was the case with Palamon. Nevertheless, Duke Theseus, who was anxious to avoid rancor and jealousy, had a herald proclaim that each side had done exactly as well as the other, as though they had been as much alike as brothers. Then he gave gifts to each of the knights and held a feast for three days together. When it was over, he traveled along with them a day's march on their homeward journey, to do them honor, and bade them a friendly farewell.

Meanwhile, however, things had not gone well with Arcite. None of the doctors could help him. The wound had been too serious for any natural healing power to take effect. There was nothing for it but that Arcite should leave this life. He sent for Emily and Palamon.

"I cannot tell you, my lady," he said painfully to Emily when the two of them had come to his bed—"I cannot express what great sorrow I feel. My spirit shall always be in your service, even when my body is dead. Alas! the pains that I have suffered for you, and the long time that I have suffered them! You are my own sweetheart, although you are the cause of my death, too. What sense is there in my life? An instant together with my beloved, and then alone, in the cold ground. Farewell, lovely Emily! Take me gently in your arms and listen to what I have to say.

"I have striven jealously with my cousin Palamon here for love of you ever since I first saw you. Yet as a true lover and a true man there is no one better in the world than Palamon, and you are the one he loves. If you are ever willing to marry, do not forget Palamon." And with these words Arcite's speech began to falter. As his heart felt the pangs of death, his senses failed. His vision grew dark and his breath nearly stopped, but he still directed his gaze at his lady. His last words were, "Mercy, Emily!" Then he was dead and cold. May his god Mars take care of his soul.

Emily gave a cry and fell into a swoon, and Theseus had to carry her away from the bedside. When she regained consciousness her mourning was constant and bitter, and so was Palamon's. The whole town of Athens gave itself over to sorrow at the death of the young Theban. Theseus' noble heart was again moved by pity and he arranged for a magnificent funeral. In the same grove where Arcite had been overheard by Palamon, he ordered great oak trees to be felled and laid one on another to make a funeral pyre. Then a bier was covered with cloth of gold, on which Arcite might be carried. His body was also dressed in cloth of gold, with a crown of evergreen laurel on his head. In his hand was laid a bright sword, as befitted a warrior. He was carried off in funeral procession toward the grove. Three great white horses came first, with men on them, carrying his shield, his spear, and his Turkish bow. Then, on foot, came the noblest of the Greeks, slowly and solemnly, carrying Arcite on his bier, their eyes red and wet with tears.

They passed through the main street, which was draped in black. At the last came Theseus, Palamon, and Emily, carrying golden vessels with honey, milk, and wine, and bearing a lighted torch to set to the funeral pyre. Arcite was laid on the huge pile of oak, and Emily, half-fainting, laid the fire to the straw beneath. Around the corpse were spices, cloth of gold, jewels, flower garlands, and incense, and all these riches were burned together in an enormous fire that blazed so fiercely it flamed above the treetops. Some people threw in their jewels, some their shields, some their spears, some their rich clothing, along with the contents of the golden vessels. The Greek soldiers rode around the fire three times, and clashed their spears together three times; then all the ladies cried out together three times. When the body was burned to ashes, the Greeks held great athletic contests in Arcite's honor, according to their custom. At last, after doing him every conceivable honor, they left and went home.

After several years had passed and the general mourning had ceased, Theseus held a great meeting of the leaders of several countries to establish peace among various lands and to place the people of Thebes under his own wise government. He wished the days of Creon to be forgotten.

Theseus sent for Palamon, who came in black, still sorrowing for his cousin Arcite. He also sent for Emily, who was still equally mournful. When all those he had summoned had gathered in one place before him he began to speak: "The world is so

arranged that everything—fire, water, earth, and air—has certain bounds beyond which it may not go. In the same way, there are bounds to everything in time, as well as in space. The sun does not stay in one place, burning us continually, but comes up and goes down according to its proper time. The oak tree lives for a long time, but finally dies; stone is worn away, and great cities disappear. Animals and men, too, have their proper time: They are born and

they die, living on only through their generations of children. This is how the world is, and there is no use struggling against it.

"Then surely it is wise to make a virtue of necessity, and cease to be unhappy over the death of Arcite. He died at a good time, when he was still at the height of strength and glory. He missed much pain by his early death. Besides, what good does it do him for Palamon and Emily to continue mourning? He would much rather have them happy. Therefore, I propose that before we leave this place we make one complete joy out of two imperfect sorrows.

"Sister Emily," he said, "you know how willingly and completely Palamon has loved you ever since he saw you. It is time for you, my sister, to take as your husband this member of the royal house of Thebes. It is a cruel woman who will not finally take pity upon a man who has loved her so long. You have seen me show mercy where I might have been cruel and hard; now I call upon you to take him in marriage, for if you do so you will knit together Athens and Thebes in peace and harmony. You will love him as he loves you, without any of the anger and jealousy that Palamon and Arcite felt toward each other. Sooner or later you will have children that are the only means we poor mortal men have of continuing our race. Palamon," he said, turning to the young knight, "I do not need to ask you for your consent; I already know what your answer will be. Come here, and take your lady by the hand."

So Palamon and Emily were married. They lived happily for a long time. Emily loved Palamon tenderly, and Palamon loved her as he always had. There was never a word of anger or jealousy in their love.

This is the end of their story, and may Heaven save all this company!

*Here Ends the Knight's Tale*

# THE WIFE OF BATH'S TALE
## The Prologue

WHEN THE KNIGHT had told his tale, there wasn't a soul in the company, young or old, who didn't say that it was a truly noble story—but of course the gentlefolk liked it particularly well.

Our Host laughed and swore, "By my soul, this is going well: the ice is broken. Let's see who ought to tell another tale now, for the game is well begun. Sir Parish Priest, you're a learned man, what about you? Tell us a story, for God's sake."

"Lord have mercy!" answered this honest parson. "What ails the man to swear so sinfully?"

Our Host answered, "Well, well—I see we're going to hear a sermon!"

"NO!" said the Wife of Bath, "This is no time for dull old sermons! Let *me* tell you a story. I can tell you a tale or two about what life is really like, and the troubles real people have here in this world. Believe me, I speak from experience."

The rest of us laughed a bit at the Wife's interruption, and nudged each other, looking at her—she presented quite a figure, in those red stockings and that huge hat. She was plainly a great talker, and it would have been no use to try and stop her.

"I've had five husbands," she went on, "and been five times widowed. All of my husbands were worthy men in their ways. But when you bring two people together, one of them has to be the manager or there will be arguments all the time. I think the wife ought to be the manager."

The Pardoner jumped up in his saddle, exclaiming, "Why, dame, I had been thinking of marrying myself; but if wives are so hard on their husbands, maybe I ought to think twice before I get married!"

"Wait until I have told my tale," she answered. "I'm an expert on marriage: soon you'll know all about it."

"Tell on," said the Pardoner, "and teach us young men some of your lore."

"Gladly," said the Wife. "Now, to tell the truth, three of my husbands were good and two were bad. The first three were good and old and rich, and believe me, I had no trouble managing them. How I made them work! They had real reason to be glad when I spoke kindly to them, for I certainly could scold them roundly; they got no peace at all until they gave me all the clothes I

wanted. But my fourth husband was a play-
boy, and made me terribly angry. I did my
best to get even with him, and punished him
sorely; but he's in his grave now, God rest
his soul. My fifth husband was most unkind
to me, and yet I loved him best of all—I
married him for love, and not for money.
I guess he was twenty years old, and I was
forty. We quarreled all the time, until one
day I tore some pages out of his book, and
he hit me on the ear: I'm still deaf from that
blow. Well, I lay as still as a stone, and he
was sure I was dying! He was very sorry
for what he had done. After that we made
it up, and he promised to obey my wishes in
everything—and we never had another bit
of trouble. Now I'll tell my tale, if you'll
listen."

At this point the Friar began laughing,
and said, "Well! This has certainly been a
long preface to a tale! When does the
story start?"

"By the bones of Saint Thomas!" cried
the Summoner. "Why must a friar be always interrupting? Be still, and stop bother-
ing us."

The Friar turned angrily, and shouted
back, "So that's what you think about
friars, do you? By my faith, I'll have a tale
or two to tell about summoners before
we're through!"

"Is that so? You just wait and hear the
stories I'm going to tell about friars—"
began the Summoner, but the Host roared
"Quiet now, both of you! Let the woman
tell her tale!"

"I'm quite ready," said the wife cheerfully, "if I have the permission of this
worthy friar?"

"Yes, indeed," said he. "Tell on, and I
shall listen."

So the Wife of Bath told a tale to explain
her ideas about marriage, and to prove that
a husband should always obey his wife.

# The Loathly Lady

In the days of King Arthur, many hundreds of years ago, this land was filled with fairies, and I have heard that there were elves behind every tree—but there aren't any more now, because the holy friars are always going around praying, to frighten the fairies away. It happened, then, that there was a young knight at the court of King Arthur, and one day he carried off a young maiden against her will. This was a crime that was punishable by death, and the people were so angry about it that there was quite an uproar. According to the law, the knight was to be beheaded.

However, the queen, together with the other ladies of the court, begged the king to turn the offender over to her, and let her determine his punishment. Finally the king agreed. He thought that a man who had hurt a woman ought to be judged by other women.

The queen assembled her ladies, and summoned the knight before her, saying: "You know that you deserve to die for your crime. But I shall grant you your life if you can tell me what thing it is that women most desire. If you can do this, your neck is safe. I give you leave to go for a year and a day to seek for the right answer, if you will swear to return at the given time."

The unhappy knight moaned and sighed, but he had no choice in the matter. He had to agree to the conditions, promising to go and return at the end of the year with whatever answer he could find. And so he went forth, stopping at every house and every possible place trying to find what thing women love most. But look where he might, he could not find any two people who could agree on an answer.

Some said women loved money best; others said honor; some said beauty; some, expensive clothes; and some said love. Some said we are most satisfied when we are flattered and waited on—and, to tell the truth, that was pretty nearly right. And some said that we love best to be free to do as we please, and never to be critized; and it certainly is true that we like to be thought wise and good, no matter what the truth is! Some said that we like to be trusted and thought discreet, and able to keep a secret. Alas, we women can't keep anything quiet!

When this knight found that he just could not find any answer, he was sadder than ever. But there was no help for it, and the time came when he had to start back home.

One day on the journey back, as he was going through a forest, he came upon a clearing where there were twenty-four ladies dancing—or perhaps even more—and he stopped, hoping that somehow they might be able to help him. But as he drew near the dancers they suddenly disappeared. He couldn't see a single living creature in the clearing, except one very old woman— the most hideous being imaginable—who was sitting on the grass. The old woman stood up before the knight, saying, "Sir knight, you have lost your way; there is no road here. Tell me what you are looking for, and perhaps it will be the better for you: old folk know many things."

"Good mother," said the knight, "I know that I am no better than dead unless I can tell what thing it is that women most desire. If you could tell me that, I would give you anything."

"Promise me, then, that you will do the next thing I ask of you, if you possibly can, and I will tell you what you wish to know at once."

"I swear it," said the knight, "by my honor."

"Then," said she, "your life is safe, for I shall keep my bargain. Upon my life, the queen will agree. There is no lady anywhere who will dare say I am wrong. Let's go on at once without any more talk." Then she whispered a sentence in his ear, and told him to be cheerful, and not to be afraid.

When they arrived at the court the knight sent word to the queen that he had kept his bargain, and had come on the appointed day, ready with his answer. Many noble wives, and many maidens, and many a widow (since widows are so wise) assembled to hear this answer. The queen herself sat as judge. The knight was called forth to tell this audience what women love best. He was not shy to answer, but spoke in a manly voice that all the court could hear: "My liege lady, generally women desire to

have sovereignty over their husbands, and to rule them. That is their greatest desire. I say this is true, even if you kill me. Now do as you please with me: I am at your mercy."

In all the court there wasn't a wife or a maid or a widow who denied what he said. They all agreed that he deserved to keep his life.

Immediately the old woman, the one whom the knight had found sitting on the grass, jumped up. "Mercy," said she, "my sovereign lady queen. Before your court departs, give me justice. I taught this answer to the knight, and in return he promised me to do the first thing I asked of him, if he possibly could." Then she turned to the knight, and continued: "In the presence of this court, I pray you, sir knight, to make me your wife, for you know very well that I have saved your life. If I speak falsely, say so."

"Alas," answered the knight, "I know well enough that that was my promise. But for the love of God, choose another request: Take all my money and goods, but let my person go."

"By no means," said she; "I may be old and ugly and poor, but unless I could be your wife and your love, I wouldn't want all the gold in the world."

"My love!" he cried. "No, my doom! Alas, to think that any member of my family should be so shamed!"

But his protests were of no use, and in the end he was forced to keep his promise and marry her.

Now, some people might say that I am to be blamed for neglecting to tell them all the interesting details of the joy and celebration at the wedding feast; but the truth is that there wasn't any joy or any feast at all. There was nothing but gloom and sorrow. He married her very privately in the morning, but he was so unhappy to have such an ugly, elderly wife that he hid himself for the rest of the day as if he were an owl.

That night, when the newly married pair were alone, the knight was so miserable he couldn't sleep. He tossed and turned and groaned—while his wife lay there quietly, smiling at him. Finally she said, "Dearest husband, do all the knights of King Arthur's court treat their wives this way? I am your own dear wife, and I have saved your life. Certainly, I never did you any wrong. Yet, you act like a man who has lost his mind. What have I done? Tell me, and if I can do anything to help matters, I will."

"Help matters!" exclaimed the knight. "If only something could be done! You are so horribly ugly, old, and of such low, peasant blood it's no wonder that I toss

miserably on my bed. I know my heart will break completely!''

"Is this," she asked, "the cause of your unhappiness?"

"Yes, of course," he answered; "naturally I'm unhappy."

"Well, sir," said she, "I could change all this in less than three days, if you behaved properly toward me. But I think your attitude is a little silly. The greatest gentleman is the man who behaves like a gentleman, not the one who is born of a noble family. The worst crimes may be committed by sons of the best families. Is it to your own credit that your family left you money, or

an honorable name, unless you keep it honorable? Most people think that it wasn't honorable for you to have carried off that young maiden. Villainous deeds make a lord a churl. Poverty, on the other hand, may make a person appreciate all the more the true gifts of God. Therefore, please do not scorn me for my poverty or lowly birth, but judge me only by my behavior. It's true that I am old and ugly, but this could be an advantage to you, because it will make it all the more sure that I will be a humble

and obliging wife, interested only in pleasing you.

"Choose, now," said she: "you may have one of two things. Either you may have me old and ugly until I die, but a true and faithful wife who will never displease you in any way; or else you may have me young and fair—and take your chances on how foolishly I may behave, and how much annoyance my youthful gaiety may cause you. It's your choice: whichever you please, it shall be so. It is within my power to change my form."

The astonished knight thought about this, and was greatly troubled. But at last, remembering some of the lessons that had been so hard to learn, he answered: "My lady and my love, my wife so dear, I put myself entirely in your power. You yourself choose whatever will be most pleasant and honorable to you, and to me also. I don't care which: whatever you desire will also please me."

"Then do I have the mastery of you," she asked, "so that I may choose to do exactly what I wish?"

"Yes, certainly, wife," said he. "I think that is best."

The lady was delighted. "Kiss me," she said. "We shall never be angry with each other again. You shall have both the gifts I offered you. I will be both fair and good. May I lose my life unless I am as good to you as ever wife was since the beginning of the world! And if I am not as beautiful to look at as any queen or empress the sun shines on, you are free to kill me if you wish. Cast up the curtain, and see if I am telling the truth."

The knight did so, and could hardly believe his eyes. Before him was a young and lovely woman, not the repulsive hag he had known. She had used fairy magic, and transformed herself.

He took his wife in his arms and kissed her, overcome with joy. Thereafter she obeyed him in everything that might add to his bliss, and thus they lived for the rest of their lives in perfect happiness.

"Now may the Lord send us all husbands, meek, young, and strong," said the Wife of Bath, "and a pestilence upon those who will not be governed by their wives!"

*Here Ends the Wife of Bath's Tale*

# THE FRIAR'S TALE
# The Prologue

THE FRIAR had been sulking, and glaring at the Summoner all during the Wife's tale, but he minded his manners and held his tongue. As soon as she was finished, he burst out: "Long life to you, dame; you dealt very well with some knotty matters. But now, if this company will permit me, I should like to tell you a funny story about a summoner. Of course, you all know very well that nothing good can possibly be said

about a summoner. When a summoner appears in any town, all the people know he is going to accuse them of crimes they never committed, and summon them to appear in court just so he can make some money out of them. Summoners are all scum, hated by young and old alike."

Our Host protested, "Dear sir, be polite and courteous, as a man of your profession should be. We don't want any quarrels in this gentle company. Tell your tale, and leave the Summoner alone."

"That's all right," said the Summoner; "let him say whatever he wants to me. I'll get even enough with him when my turn comes. I'll let him know what a great honor it is to be a lying, oily beggar of a friar."

"Peace!" cried our Host, "no more of this!" Turning to the Friar, he added: "Tell your tale, my master."

# The Devil and the Summoner

There was once a judge in my part of the country who was famous for his severity in punishing all the crimes that came to his attention. Those who were accused of witchcraft, or not paying the church taxes, or breaking contracts had every reason to shake in their boots if they were summoned to appear in his court. The fines he imposed were likely to take a lifetime's savings.

This judge employed a summoner, whose job was to detect all wrongdoers, and to force them to appear at court. The summoner was certainly a master at his trade. He had a spy system which reached to every corner of the county, and every one of his spies reported personally and secretly to the summoner. Of course, the summoner never took half this information to his master, the judge. It paid him much better to blackmail the accused persons, and keep all the money he could get from them for himself.

It was very easy for him to do this, since all he had to do was to go to the accused person with a warrant for his arrest, saying something like this: "Friend, for your sake I shall do all I can to hush this matter up, and see that it never reaches the judge's ears. But I'll have to go to a great deal of trouble to silence the witnesses, who are sure to demand plenty of money. Of course

you know I'm not a rich man—far from it—but for the sake of your friendship I would like to help, if I could." And, of course, even if there was not a word of truth in the accusation, the victim knew he'd better pay the summoner every penny he could scrape up, or else the false thief of a summoner would summon him to court, where the chances were that the fine would be ten times worse. This summoner knew more about how to get bribes than I could possibly tell you even if I took two years to do it.

Thus it happened that one day the summoner, always on the watch for a new victim, rode out, heading for the cottage of an elderly widow. He intended to summon her to court on a false charge so that he could get a bribe from her. As he rode along through the forest he saw a man he did not know riding ahead of him. The stranger was a merry yeoman carrying a bow and arrows, and he was dressed in bright green. This was odd, because no one but fairies and outlaws wore green usually, but of course the summoner, being a bold thief himself, wasn't afraid of outlaws. As for fairies and such creatures, he had often said that he wouldn't be afraid of the devil himself.

The summoner hailed the man in green, and spurred his horse to catch up with him. The stranger turned, saying, "Welcome, friend! Where are you riding, here in this deep wood? Must you go far today?"

"No," answered the summoner, "my errand is quite nearby. I'm going to collect some money for my lord."

"Are you an estate-manager then?" asked the stranger.

"That's right," said the summoner. "I supervise my lord's estates and collect his rents. I am a bailiff." He did not dare, for

very shame, admit that he was a summoner, because he knew that everyone hated the very word.

"Why that's interesting," the man in green remarked. "I'm a bailiff myself, dear brother. But I am a stranger in this part of the world. I am most delighted to meet you, and hope I can consider you a brother from now on. I have plenty of gold and silver at home, and it is all at your service if you ever happen to come to our country."

"Splendid!" exclaimed the summoner, and they shook hands, swearing to be brothers for the rest of their lives. Thus they rode on, conversing and joking together. The summoner was as full of gossip as a snake is of venom, and he was forever asking questions. He now inquired, "My brother, where is this home of yours, in case I should be looking for you sometime?"

The stranger answered, "It is directly south of here, quite some distance away. I certainly hope to see you there soon. Before we part, I'll give you such clear directions on how to get there that you couldn't possibly miss your way."

"Now, brother," said this summoner, "since you, too, are a bailiff, won't you teach me some of your tricks as we ride along? Tell me how I can succeed and grow as prosperous as you. Don't bother about whether it's legal or honest, but tell me, as my sworn brother, how you manage."

"To tell the truth, dear brother," answered the man in green, "my wages are pitifully small. My lord is very severe, a hard man to work for, and my duties are extremely taxing. Therefore I have to get along as best I may by dishonest dealings. In fact, I take all that men will give me. Whether I have to get it by trickery or by violence, I manage somehow to get everything that I want from year to year. I'm afraid that's the way it is."

"Indeed!" exclaimed the summoner, "it's just the same with me! I don't hesitate to take anything—unless it's too heavy to lift or too hot to carry. Anything I can get in secret never bothers *my* conscience. If it weren't for such robbery, I couldn't live at all. It doesn't bother me at all if it's sinful. We are well met, by the Lord Harry! But tell me your name, dear brother."

The man in green had a rather odd smile on his face. "Brother," he asked, "do you really want to know? I am a demon. My home is in Hell. I am here to do a little collecting—to see whether men will give me anything. You ride around in order to get some profit for yourself; I do exactly the same thing. I would ride to the end of the world for a victim."

"Bless us!" cried the summoner. "I really thought you were an ordinary yeoman! You have a man's body, just like mine. Do you always have the same shape, when you are at home in Hell?"

"No, certainly not," answered the demon in green. "There we have no particular shape, but we can take one whenever we like. Sometimes I go about as a man, sometimes as an ape, or even an angel. There's nothing very strange about that. Any man that takes rabbits out of hats can make you think you see something that isn't there, and I have far more skill than he has."

"But why," asked the summoner, "do you go about in various different shapes, rather than keeping one?"

"Because," the demon answered, "we like to take whatever form will help us most to snare our victims."

"And why do you go to all this trouble?"

"Ah, there are many reasons, dear summoner," answered the demon. "But this is not the time to tell them to you. The day is getting on. Here it is noon, and I haven't gained a thing yet today. I'd better attend

to business, and leave this talk until later. Actually, my brother, you couldn't understand, even if I had time to tell you all our reasons."

"Yet tell me truly," said the summoner, "how are you able to make all these new bodies for yourselves?"

"Well," said the demon, "sometimes, of course, we just pretend to have bodies. At other times, we can use the bodies of the dead. But, quite seriously, I assure you that you shall find out all about it hereafter, my dear brother. The time will come when you won't have to learn it from me. What you'll see for yourself will teach you more about this sort of thing than you could learn from any professor or learned clerk alive. Now let's hurry on. I'd like to stay with you, unless you see fit to leave me."

"Don't worry," said this summoner. "I'm not going to leave you. I always keep my word. Even if you were Satan himself, I would keep my pledge of brotherhood to you. Let's go on about our business together. As long as there's money in it, I would as soon have a demon for a brother

as any man. You take your share, whatever men will give you, and I'll take mine. That way we'll both profit. If either of us gets more than the other, let him keep his promise and share it with his brother."

"I'll be glad to agree to that," said the demon.

And with that they went along their way. When they drew near the town where the summoner wished to go, they saw a cart piled high with hay, which a carter had been driving down the road. But the road was deep with mud, and the cart was stuck. The carter, striking his horses furiously, shouted, "Hup, Scot! Hup, Dobbin! What are you stopping for? May hell take you, both body and bones! You've never been anything but trouble to me! To the Devil with you—horses, cart, and hay as well!"

The summoner said to himself, "Now we'll have some fun!" Drawing close to his demon comrade, he nudged him, and whispered in his ear, "Listen, brother: did you hear what that carter said? Take his hay and his cart, as well as his horses—he has given them to you!"

"Oh no," said the demon, "not a bit of it. He didn't mean it, I know. Ask him yourself, if you don't believe me. Or just wait a moment, and you'll see."

Meanwhile the carter stroked his horses' necks, and they began to draw and pull. "Hup, now!" he cried. "God bless you! Well done, my loves! May the Lord preserve you!" and the cart slowly pulled out of the mud.

"See, brother," said the demon, "what did I tell you? Here you can see that the carter said one thing, but he thought another. I can only take those things that are freely given. Let's go on—there's nothing to be gained here."

When they reached the end of the town, the summoner confided to his brother, "In this house lives an old widow who'd almost rather lose her neck than part with a single penny. Yet I'll get a shilling from her, or summon her to defend herself in court, although goodness knows I know no evil of her. Since you don't seem to be making much headway in this part of the country, watch closely and follow my example."

Then the summoner knocked loudly at the widow's door, crying, "Come on out, you old hag! I bet you're up to no good in there."

"Who is knocking so?" asked the old widow. She came to the door carrying the pan in which she had been cooking her supper. "Bless you, sir, what do you want?"

"I have a bill of summons," said he. "See that you are in court first thing tomorrow morning to answer certain grave charges against you."

"Now God help me," she exclaimed, "I can't possibly do that! I have been sick for many days, and I could never walk that far, or even ride. I have such a pain in my side, it would kill me. Can't you tell me what the charge is, so that I may ask someone to represent me there and defend me?"

"Well," said the summoner, "if you'll pay me a shilling at once I'll get you off. It won't be enough to do me much good. My master gets all the profit, not I. Come on now, and let me move on. Give me a shilling, I can't wait here all night."

"A shilling!" she cried. "By Our Lady, I couldn't find a shilling to save my soul! I don't see that much money from one year's end to another. You know that I am poor and old; show mercy to me, poor wretch that I am."

"Certainly not," he answered. "May the devil fetch me if I let you off for a penny less, even if it kills you!"

"Alas," she wept, "I know I'm not guilty of anything."

"Pay me," said he, "or by Saint Anne, I'll take away your new pan to cover a debt you have long owed me. That time you were caught stealing from the convent garden I paid your fine for you." With that, he grabbed her pan from her hands.

"You lie!" she said. "Never in my life was I summoned to your court before now.

And never did I take so much as a radish dishonestly!" She dropped to her knees and shook her fist. "I wish the devil would take you—and my pan, too!"

When the demon heard her curse so, he said to her gently, "Now, my dear, is this really your wish?"

She answered promptly, "May the devil carry him off alive, pan and all, unless he repents!"

"No chance of that, you old sow," said this summoner. "I wouldn't dream of repenting! Not for anything you could give me—although I'd gladly take everything you own, even the rags on your back."

"Now, brother," said the demon, who had been waiting for the old lady to ask this all along, "don't be angry: you and the pan are mine by right. She has given you both to me. You shall go with me to Hell tonight, and then you'll see that my promises will be fulfilled. You'll learn more about Hell and its ways than any doctor of divinity knows."

And with these words, the demon grabbed him, and took him, body and soul, to the place where all summoners belong.

"May God save us," finished the Friar, "and may He help these summoners to become good men."

*Here Ends the Friar's Tale*

The Summoner stood up high in his stirrups. He was so angry at the Friar that he shook like an aspen leaf. "My lords," he said, "the Friar boasts that he knows all about Hell—and well he may. Friars and fiends are birds of a feather, everyone knows that. I've heard that the very worst part of Hell is reserved for friars, and it must be awfully crowded."

So the Summoner went on insulting the Friar until the Host, hoping to stop the wrangling and restore order, turned hastily to the Clerk.

# THE CLERK'S TALE
# The Prologue

"SIR CLERK OF OXFORD," said our Host, "you ride as shyly and quietly as a young girl going to her wedding. I haven't heard a word from you all day long. I guess your mind is busy with some learned problem, but there's a time and a place for everything. Look alive, for heaven's sake—this is no time for deep thought. Tell us some merry tale now, according to our agreement. Don't tell us some long, dismal sermon, like a preacher in Lent trying to make us repent our sins, and don't go telling some dull thing that will put us to sleep. Make it full of fun and adventure. And you can keep all your long words and learned terms for writing to the other clerks at the university. Right now, use plain English."

The Clerk answered courteously, "I am at your command, Host, and will do my best to obey you. I will tell you a tale I learned in Italy from Francis Petrarch, a most learned clerk."

# Patient Griselda

There is a province called Saluzzo in the western part of Italy, where you can still see towers and towns built a great many years ago. A duke once was lord of that land, as his fathers had been before him. He lived an easy and happy life, beloved and obeyed by all the people of the country, both lords and common people. This young lord's name was Walter. He was fair and young and strong, honorable and courteous, and, for the most part, wise. In some respects, however, he wasn't as wise as he might have been, for he gave little thought to the future. He cared only for the pleasures of the moment, giving all his energy to hawking and hunting. He let just about everything else slide. Worst of all, he would not consider taking a wife on any account.

His people were so unhappy about this state of affairs that one day a great group of them came to court to see the duke. Their appointed spokesman said, on behalf of all the people of the land, "Noble duke, we hope you will forgive us for daring to speak so to you, but we, your people, are deeply worried. If you will only listen to us, that is all we ask. We know, gentle lord, that we could not ask for a better ruler. All is so well in our land that we could scarcely ask for any improvement, except, lord, for one thing. We are afraid that you might die without an heir, leaving the land to fall into the hands of strangers. Therefore, we pray you to marry in all haste. If you agree, we will be happy to choose you a bride from among the greatest and most noble families in the land."

The duke, moved by their concern, answered, "My dear subjects, you ask me to do a thing I never dreamed of doing. I have always dreaded the servitude of marriage, and rejoiced in my liberty. But I understand your worry, and I will follow your advice. Of my own free will, I shall be married as soon as possible. But I ask you to withdraw your offer to find me a wife. A wife from among the most noble families of the land may not necessarily be the best wife. Let me choose my wife myself. I charge you solemnly to assure me that you will welcome and honor, as long as she may live, whatever wife I choose, just as if she were the daughter of an emperor. Furthermore, I must ask you to promise that you shall never grumble or complain about my choice. If I must give up my freedom at your request, I wish to marry where I choose. Unless you will agree to this, I shall have to ask you to speak no more of the matter."

They agreed at once, but asked, before they went, that he set a definite date for his

marriage then and there, so that the people could be sure that he would really take a wife. He named a day, and they went their ways thankfully, their purpose accomplished. At once the duke called his servants, telling them to prepare all things for the marriage feast.

Not far from the splendid palace where the duke was planning his wedding there stood a little village whose inhabitants were hard-working peasants. They were poor, but they lived contentedly within their means. Among these poor folk lived a man, whose name was Janicula, who was the poorest of them all. But although Janicula

beauty of this humble maiden. But, beyond her beauty, he especially admired her quiet, grave expression, and her goodness, extraordinary in one so young. Considering these things, he made a secret resolution that if he should ever marry he would marry only Griselda.

Now the day of the wedding drew close, but no one had any idea who the bride would be. The people wondered greatly, whispering to each other, "What is our lord thinking of? Isn't he going to marry after all?" But meanwhile the duke ordered many precious stones set in gold and azure to make necklaces and bracelets and rings, and they were all for Griselda. He had rich robes made in her size, and all the other adornments suitable for a royal bride.

The morning of the day when the wedding was to take place the palace was decorated gaily, the tables piled high with all sorts of rare and delicious foods from all over Italy. The royal duke, in his wedding garments, then led the procession of all the lords and ladies who had been invited to the feast straight to the village where Griselda lived.

Griselda, of course, had no idea of the duke's intentions, and she went about her daily duties just as usual. But of course she had heard that the wedding was to take place that day, and she thought she would dearly love to catch a glimpse of the bride. She thought about this as she came home from the village well, carrying her jug of water. She walked fast, thinking that she would have more time to watch for the royal couple if she got her chores done as quickly as possible. But just as she was about to re-enter her cottage, the duke rode up and called to her. She quickly set down her jug and dropped to her knees before him, waiting quietly to hear what her lord had to say.

was poor and humble, he had a special treasure in his home, a good and beautiful daughter whose name was Griselda. Griselda was very young, but she was also wise and loving, and she cared tenderly for her old father. She had never known any luxuries. Her life was one of hard work, with never an idle moment until bedtime. All day she spun as she watched over the sheep, and on her way home in the evening she collected herbs and greens to cook for her father's dinner. Her first thought was always to make him comfortable and happy.

Many times the duke had ridden through this village, and he had noticed the great

The duke spoke solemnly, saying, "Where is your father, Griselda?" She answered, humbly, "My lord, he is here."

Without a moment's delay, she went inside and sent her father to the duke, who took the old man by the hand and, taking him to one side, said, "Janicula, if you will consent, I wish to take your daughter as my wife, to care for her as long as she lives."

This was so sudden and unexpected that the astonished old man blushed and shook so that he could scarcely stand. He managed to stammer in answer: "Lord, whatever you wish is also my desire. You are my dear lord, and it shall be as you say."

"Yet," said the duke softly, "Let me consult with you and your daughter in your room. I wish to ask her if she will be my wife, and be guided by me. This should be done in your presence."

Janicula agreed, and they went into the room where Griselda waited. She turned pale with astonishment at the sight of so lordly a guest in her humble cottage—as well she might.

"Griselda," said the duke, "it is your father's and my desire that I marry you, and so it shall be, if, as I suppose, you so wish. But first I must ask you a question or two. Since the marriage must be performed at once, you must say whether you will agree or not.

"I ask you this: Are you ready to do cheerfully whatever I wish, so that I may always act as seems best to me? Can I make you either happy or unhappy without your ever grumbling at any time? Will you, when I say 'yea,' never say 'nay,' either by words or frowns? Swear to this, and I swear you shall be my wife."

Trembling with fear, and struck with complete wonder, she answered, "Lord, I am quite unworthy of such an honor. But your wishes are mine, and I swear that I will never willingly disobey you in thought or deed."

"This is enough, my Griselda," said he, and he led her to the door. To the people waiting outside he said: "This is the wife I have chosen. Honor and love her, if you love me."

The duke did not want Griselda to bring any of her shabby old possessions to his palace, so he ordered his ladies to disrobe her right there. The fine ladies of the court did not at all want to touch Griselda's old rags, but they obeyed, and clothed the lovely young maiden in new clothes from head to foot. When they had combed out her flowing hair, they set a crown on her head and decked her with all manner of precious jewels. When they were through she was so transformed by her new finery that people could scarcely recognize her as the same person.

The duke married her on the spot. He set her on his snow-white horse, and off they rode to the palace, cheered by the joyful people.

The new duchess was so lovely and gracious that it seemed impossible that she could have been raised in a cottage. She quickly became so loved and worshiped by everyone that even people who had known her from her birth could hardly believe that she was Janicula's daughter. She, who had always been good, seemed to become more so every day. She won the hearts of all: her fame spread far and wide, and men and women came from all around the countryside to gaze on her.

Thus the duke's marriage brought him peace and joy at home, and the approval of all his land. Since he had seen that virtue may be hidden in the most wretched hut, people admired his wisdom and prudence, and praised him highly.

In due time Griselda's first child, a daughter, was born, to the great joy of the duke and the people. But unfortunately this joy was not to last long, for while this child was still a tiny infant the duke was overcome with a great longing to test his wife's loyalty, and he simply could not get this thought from his mind. He had every reason to know that she was always good, patient, and loyal, for he had been testing her in little ways all during their life together. Still, he could not resist the needless desire to test her again and again.

Therefore he came to her one night with a grim face, saying: "Griselda, do you remember that I took you away from rags and poverty and made you a duchess? I expect you haven't forgotten. Now listen to me carefully: Although you are very dear to me, you are not in the least dear to my nobles. They grumble behind your back, saying that it is shameful to be your sub-

jects, when you were born a mere peasant. I'm afraid that the complaints have multiplied since your daughter was born. You know that I must be very careful, and do what is best for all—not as I wish, but as my people demand. This is most painful to me, but I do not wish to act without your knowledge. I expect you to obey me and agree in this matter, and show the patience and obedience you promised me in your village on our wedding day."

Griselda heard all this without appearing disturbed or grieved, and answered, "Lord, we are at your pleasure. My child and I are yours; you may save or ruin what is your own. Do as you wish. Nothing you want could displease me, for there is nothing I wish, or fear to lose, except only yourself. Your will shall always be my desire. Neither time nor death will change my feelings."

The duke was delighted with her answer, but he pretended to be very miserable, and as he left her he sighed deeply. He then went and explained his plan to a soldier whom he trusted, sending the soldier to Griselda's room.

"Madame," said this soldier, "forgive me, but I must carry out my lord's orders. I am commanded to take this child."

With that, he grabbed the baby roughly, looking as if he were going to kill it. Griselda sat as meek as a lamb. She was afraid he would slay her beloved daughter, yet she neither wept nor sighed, in accordance with her promise never to protest against her husband's decisions. All that she asked was to kiss her child before it died. Taking it in her lap, she rocked and kissed it, saying, "Farewell, my child, I shall never see you again." Then she turned to the soldier, saying, "Go now, and do as my lord commands."

He took the child and carried it to the duke. When he had reported every word Griselda had said, telling of every detail of her expression and tone of voice, the duke was moved by pity, but he nevertheless was determined to have his own way and carry out his plan. He therefore told the soldier to take the baby secretly to Bologna, where his brother-in-law, the earl of Panico, lived. He told him to ask the earl and his wife to bring up the child in a manner appropriate to her rank, but never to tell anyone whose child she was.

The soldier did as he was told, and the duke sat back to see how his wife would react. But try as he might, he could not see any change in her. She was just as cheerful, humble, kind, and loving as ever, and she never once mentioned her daughter again.

Four years passed quietly, at the end of which Griselda gave birth to another child, a son. The whole land rejoiced at the birth of the heir, and indeed he was a fine, beautiful baby. But when the little boy was two years old the duke was again possessed by a great desire to test his wife's patience and loyalty, and he went to her, saying, "Wife, you have already heard how my people grumble at our marriage, and now that we have a son it is worse then ever. Their complaints reach me from every side. They say, 'When the duke is gone, we shall be ruled by the descendants of Janicula, Griselda's peasant father.' Now I'm afraid I must bow to their feelings, and dispose of our son as I did of his sister. Be patient, I beg you."

Griselda replied, "Whatever you desire is, of course, my desire, as it has always been. I do not grieve at the death of my son and daughter—at your command, I mean. You are our lord. Just as I left behind my old clothes when I accepted yours, I left behind my will and freedom. I will gladly do anything that will please you. I would gladly die even, if that would please you. Death is not so important as your love."

When the duke saw the constancy of his wife he was struck with wonder. He made a long face as he left, but he was secretly pleased.

Again he sent the soldier to take away the child. Again Griselda bore it in patience, and the soldier took the child in strictest secrecy to the earl in Bologna. And again the duke could find no change in his wife. He might have come to the conclusion that she did not love her children, but he knew very well that this was not true. Next to himself, she loved her children best.

Of course, the duke had not been telling the truth when he told Griselda that the people were complaining against her and her children. She was very well loved indeed. It was he who became very unpopular with his people. They whispered that he must be a very cruel man indeed to have murdered his own children. He could not help realizing that the people, who had once loved him, were now turning against him—but nothing could persuade him to give up his cruel and needless testing of his wife.

Some years later, when the duke's daughter was of marriageable age, he proceeded to carry out the rest of his plan to test Griselda. He wrote secretly to the earl of Panico, instructing him to send back his two children, but to tell no one whose children they were. The girl was to come adorned as a bride.

He went to Griselda, telling her that his people demanded that he take another wife. "I would have preferred to have you," he said, "but a lord cannot always do as he pleases. Already my new wife is on her way here, so I must ask you to leave. You may take the dowry you brought with you and return to your father's house."

She answered patiently, "I shall obey you gladly. Returning to my father, I shall live with him the rest of my life as if I were a widow. Certainly I could never be the wife of another man. But as for my dowry, I know I brought you nothing, not even the clothes on my back. I shall certainly return all the clothes you have given me, and the jewels—even my wedding ring. But I trust you will not make me go without even a smock to wear on my way."

"Take the smock you are wearing," said he, and promptly she stripped off all her jewels and fine robes, down to her smock. Wearing nothing but this, she walked barefoot toward her father's house. As she walked, the people followed weeping, but she went dry-eyed, and never said a word. Her old father, Janicula, had heard the news and he hurried out to meet his daughter. Folding her in his arms, he wept bitterly. He had brought along her old dress, but too many years had passed and it would no longer fit.

Now for a time Griselda lived quietly with her father, just as she had done in her youth, and she showed no sign that she had ever lived in any other way. She worked as hard as before, and was always quiet, cheerful, and humble. But when the earl of Panico arrived from Bologna with the two young people, the duke sent for Griselda. She came to his court, and dropped on her knees before him to hear what his wishes might be. "Griselda," said he, "I wish my new bride to be received with all royal honors, but there is no one here who knows how to manage my household the way you do. You know just the way I like to have everything. Therefore, although you look a disgrace in your shabby clothing, I want you to take care of all this for me."

"I am always happy to serve and please you in any way I may," said Griselda. "I shall never cease to love and honor you, and to strive to please you."

So Griselda set to work to put the palace in order, urging the servants to hurry at their work. She made sure that every room was beautifully decked for the new bride.

She was not in the least ashamed of her ragged condition, but did her job cheerfully, and joined the rest of the court in a warm welcome to the two young people.

When dinnertime came that night, and all the nobles were sitting at the table, the duke called to Griselda, who was supervising the serving of the meal. "Griselda," he said, as if he were joking, "how do you like my pretty new wife?"

"Very well indeed," she said. "She is very beautiful. I hope you will be very happy."

When the duke saw that she said this cheerfully, and quite without malice, his heart went out to her. He lept up and said: "This is enough, my Griselda. Do not be unhappy any more. I have tried your faith and patience as much as ever a woman was tried, and I have found you always patient, faithful, and steadfast. Now I know your constancy, dear wife—" and he took her in his arms and kissed her.

Griselda could hardly believe her ears. The duke continued, "You are my wife, Griselda. I have no other. This is not my bride, but your own daughter, and her young brother is your son, my heir. Take them back—you have lost no children. I had them cared for privately at Bologna. I certainly did not kill my own children, as some people say. I only wanted to test you."

When Griselda heard this, and understood that her children were still alive, she fainted from pure joy. There was much fuss, much kissing and so forth, when she revived. As soon as possible the ladies took her off and robed her royally in cloth of gold, and put a jeweled crown on her head. When they led her back to the banquet hall there was even greater joy and feasting than there had been on her wedding day.

From that day on, the duke and Griselda lived together in peace and happiness, and all went well in their kingdom as long as they lived.

*Here Ends the Clerk's Tale*

"The moral of this story," said the Clerk, "is not that all wives should be as humble as Griselda—none of us could stand that. It is, rather, that everyone should bear difficulties as patiently as she did. But one word, lords, before I go. It would be very hard nowadays to find even one or two Griseldas in a whole town. Griselda is dead, and her patience with her. Both are buried in Italy these many years. No husband now should be so bold as to test his wife's patience, hoping to find a Griselda, for certainly he will not succeed.

"Let us honor the Wife of Bath, and all the other wives who know how to manage their husbands. I wish them long life and absolute rule. You noble, prudent wives, don't let humility nail down your tongues. You wives that are strong as elephants, don't let the men get away with anything. You know how to defend yourselves. And you wives that are weak and slender, be fierce as Indian tigers, and don't be afraid of your husbands—your tongues will subdue them fast enough!"

When the Clerk had thus ended his tale, our Host said, "By heaven, I'd give a barrel of ale if my own wife could hear that tale! She's as true as steel—but what a tongue that woman has! She doesn't know the meaning of patience. But I'd better not say any more about her. If I gave you a list of all the things that are wrong with her, somebody in this company would be sure to tell her about it when we get back to my inn. I'm a dangerous man with a dagger, but I can't stand up to my wife. I don't need to tell you who would be likely to inform on me: women are great gossips, and you know which woman here is the biggest gossip of all."

# THE FRANKLIN'S TALE
# The Prologue

BEFORE THE HOST could say any more, another pilgrim spoke up—the white-haired Franklin, who was a rich farmer and a great landholder. "By my faith, Sir Clerk," he said, "you have told your story with real wit and feeling! I have a son about your age, but he is not as sensible as you are. I could almost wish that you were in his place! All

he can do is play dice and waste all his money and spend his time talking nonsense with all the other loafers. I've had to rebuke him time and again, and I'd give a thousand pounds' worth of land to have him be a really worthy man like you."

"Straw for your worthiness!" roared the Host. "Don't you remember that every one

of us has to tell a story? Get on with yours, and stop your blathering!"

"Very well," replied the Franklin humbly. "Yes, I do remember our promise to tell stories. But please don't scorn me if I say just a word or two more to the Clerk.

"Sir Clerk, even though I admired your story, I don't think it is the last word on true virtue and gentle love. As a matter of fact, the story I want to tell has much to do with gentle love and with being a true gentleman, although there's a lot of foul magic in it, too. There's only one thing I have to

tell you before I start. I'm just a simple man, not a scholarly one like the Clerk. I can't really tell a tale as beautifully as he can. Flowery talk, alas, is above me; the only flowers I know grow on the ground. But I can tell you a story that was first told long ago, in the time of the ancient Armoricans in Brittany, where the cliffs look out over the sea. They used to sing their stories or read them for fun just as we do today."

"Get on with it," grumbled Harry Bailey, and the Franklin did so. He told his story much better than he said he could.

# The Black Rocks of Brittany

In Brittany, in the old days, there was a knight named Arveragus who was so much in love with a very noble and beautiful lady that he undertook many mighty enterprises in her honor and tried his best to win her favor. The lady's name was Dorigen, and besides being beautiful and noble, she was kind and good. Arveragus thought she was so wonderful that he was almost afraid to tell her of his love and of the distress he felt because he did not have her for his wife. After a time, she began to pity his sorrow, and then she fell in love with him, and the two of them were betrothed.

Unhappily for both of them, however, Arveragus had already promised to go off to England for a year to win more honor in feats of arms. This was his duty as a knight, and Dorigen and Arveragus both knew he must keep his promise, although she sorrowed at the very thought. They agreed that they must put off the marriage until after his return.

Before Arveragus left, however, he and Dorigen had a conversation about how things should be between them. Arveragus said, "My own lady, I love you so, that I shall never tell you what you must do after you are my wife, any more than I have done as a suitor. I shall follow your will in all things, and never feel jealous of you."

But Dorigen, knowing that love was not just a matter of one person's obeying another, replied, "Dearly beloved, I too, promise to do all things for your comfort and pleasure. I intend always to be your loving and obedient wife, and to avoid any cause of strife between us." And they both

rightly expected that they would be very happy, because their plan of being patient and gentle towards each other is the only way to make love and marriage work—whatever the Clerk and our dear companion the Wife of Bath have to say on the subject. When only one person has to do all the obeying, love can't last very long.

Arveragus sadly took leave of his lady. He sailed away in a boat from the rocky shore of Brittany to England, to keep his promise, although he dearly wished to stay near his Dorigen.

Dorigen herself nearly died for sorrow after he had gone. She stayed in her chamber all the time, and her only consolations were the frequent letters from Arveragus. Finally, however, her friends and ladies said to her, "Dear Dorigen, we are terribly worried at the way you are pining away. At least come outside sometimes, to see some different things and take your mind off your sorrows." Reluctantly, she consented, and even got in the habit of walking along the high cliffs on the seacoast where, hundreds

of feet below, the cruel waves come rushing in and break among the rocks. But this really only made her sadder. She would look at the boats coming into port and wish that Arveragus was on one of them, but then she would say to herself, "Suppose a boat carrying him were crushed by those black rocks sticking up out of the heaving water? There they are, and there is no way in the world of getting rid of them. How terrible that such dangerous obstacles should be allowed to exist!"

One day her friends persuaded her to come away from the sea, where she only grew more sorrowful, and go into a beautiful garden nearby, where people whom they knew were singing, dancing, and picnicking all the long day through, and where there seemed to be no sorrow or danger at all. It was the spring of the year, in May, and the leaves had just turned light green. Her friends thought such a place would cure her sorrow, but strange to say, Dorigen, not seeing her Arveragus in the circle of dancers, was unhappy even there.

Among the dancers, however, there was another man, a squire, almost as handsome as Arveragus. His name was Aurelius, and he sang and danced better than all the others. He was a very fine man, and he seemed as fresh and joyous as the month of May itself. But he had a secret that Dorigen didn't know: He was in love with her, too, and had been for a long time, but he had never dared to tell her so. He had made up songs about her to tell of the pain and woe of his love, but he never mentioned her name in them, so that his secret was kept from everyone. There in the garden they happened to start talking together, and Aurelius finally got up heart to say to her, "Your Arveragus has gone over the sea, but I wish that I had gone to the place from which no one returns. The reason is that I love you so! Can't you have mercy on me, and love me? A single word from you can slay or save me!" He said this, even though he knew that Dorigen was engaged to Arveragus.

Dorigen was astonished to hear him talk this way. She had not suspected before that Aurelius had this secret. But now, like a good and faithful woman, she replied, "Aurelius, if I had known you felt this way, I wouldn't have talked to you. I am betrothed, and I belong fully to Arveragus. I shall have nothing further to do with you, and that is my final word."

But then she went on to add something else. "Do you know those black rocks jutting up from the sea along the coast?" she asked him. "If you will remove every one of them, so that they don't keep a single ship from getting past, then I will be your love, and not any other way. I make you this promise, on my honor."

"But that's impossible," Aurelius said sadly and humbly. "Isn't there any other way of winning your favor?"

"I know it's impossible, Aurelius," she replied. "Otherwise I wouldn't have promised you. And no, there isn't any other way: I've already told you. You should not ask me, when I already belong to Arveragus."

Aurelius turned away from her and went home sorrowfully. Dorigen and her friends stayed in the garden until sundown, roaming up and down among the rows of flowering bushes.

All that night Aurelius lay tossing and turning in his bed. "How can I remove all the rocks from the sea?" he moaned to himself. "Nothing is more impossible. Yet if I do not do it, I shall never have Dorigen, and without her, I know I must die." He even prayed to the heathen gods of the sun and the moon to raise tides in the sea that would cover the rocks, or to bury them deep beneath the earth, but of course that didn't do any good.

For months on end he went on this way, falling more and more into despair because of his great love. He told what was ailing him to no one but his brother, who loved him dearly. This brother, who was a learned clerk and a student at the university, puzzled again and again over how the rocks could be made to vanish. The task seemed just as impossible to him as it did to Aurelius, until one day he thought of an excellent plan.

He had once studied many dark mysteries and black magic, although he was not a magician himself. He was really a law student, and he had read about magic when he should have been concentrating on his law, the way young students do. It occurred to him that there might be some magical way to make it appear that the rocks actually had been taken away. So he said to Aurelius, "Let's go to the university. Perhaps we can find some old fellow who knows enough magic to accomplish the task, so that Dorigen will have to keep her promise. The rocks wouldn't have to disappear for more than a week or two."

Aurelius was overjoyed at the idea, and the two of them set off immediately for the university in the distant city of Orleans. When their journey was almost at an end, and they were approaching the city, they met a mysterious stranger strolling down the road. To the amazement of the two brothers, he immediately said to them, "I know by my magical arts what has brought you here. You desire to make the rocks disappear from the sea on the coast of your country, so that you may gain the love of a lady, and you are seeking a magician to per-

form your task. I am a magician, and I can do what you wish."

Of course Aurelius and his brother were delighted. They got down off their horses and went along with the magician to his house. There the magician showed them his arts. Before they went to supper, he made them imagine that they saw all sorts of wonderful things that were not really there. First he made them see a huge forest full of the finest and largest wild deer that have ever been seen. Then he made the brothers see how a hundred of the deer were caught in a great hunt, with all the swift hunting dogs and their masters. Then he made them see hawks hunting heron for their masters

on a fair river; then knights fighting in a mock battle, called a joust, on a fair, smooth field. Then he made the delighted Aurelius believe he was dancing with Dorigen. At the last he suddenly clapped his hands, saying mysteriously, "Our revels now are ended," and the brothers realized that all the time they had seen these things they had been sitting alone with the magician in his study, and had not stirred a foot.

The brothers were now convinced that the magician really could make the rocks seem to go away, and they sat down to supper with him to talk about how much money he would want to do it. He made difficulties, saying, "I couldn't do it for less than a thousand pounds, and even then it's hardly worth my while."

But Aurelius was so blissful at the idea of getting Dorigen that he replied, "Fie on a thousand pounds! I'd give you the whole wide world, if I could, to perform this task. You shall have your money. I promise it on my word of honor. But what are we waiting for? I want to leave for home tomorrow morning at the latest. Be sure you are ready to come with us then." The magician agreed, and in the morning they set out for Aurelius' home, back in Brittany, where the magician immediately got to work on making the rocks seem to go away.

It was a very difficult matter, but he knew much ancient lore of astrology, and what the effects are, on earth, of the different positions of the stars and the planets. He knew, besides, that the tides in the sea, which would come up to hide part of the rocks and help his task, were controlled by the position of the moon and sun in the sky. So he got out his astronomical tables and calculated in a very complicated way just where the moon and the sun would be in relation to the stars when he wanted to work his magic. When everything was

ready, and the positions of all the heavenly bodies were just right, and he had fitted his magic carefully to them, then he did exactly what he was supposed to do, without the slightest error. Every one of the rocks disappeared from the sight of men, and he

knew that they would stay that way for a week or two.

Meanwhile, however, news had come to Dorigen that Arveragus was finally about to return from England, and plans were being made for a most sumptuous and elaborate wedding for the two of them. Of course Dorigen was almost overcome with joy, for naturally she did not know the dark plans of Aurelius and the magician. In fact, just as the rocks disappeared she had gone to the temple of the heathen gods to pray for the safe return of Arveragus.

Aurelius was in despair after he, too, learned that Arveragus was about to come home. But now the magician told him that the rocks had been disposed of. He was so delighted that he fell to his knees to give thanks to the goddess of love. Then, as quickly as he could, he ran to the temple where he knew that he would find Dorigen alone. Approaching her fearfully and humbly, he said, "Dorigen, you must know that I would never cause you displeasure if I could help it, but I love you so much that I must speak to you again about the promise that you once made to me. I don't de-

mand that you keep it, for that would be an ungentle deed. All I ask is that you remember one thing: Only by honoring your word can you keep your honesty. You promised to give me your love if I performed a certain task. The task has been accomplished. The rocks are gone! I shall be waiting, later, in the garden to see whether you keep your promise."

And with that he left the temple, not saying another word.

Dorigen was in despair at this sudden turn in her fortunes. She loved only Arveragus, most tenderly, and wanted to marry him. But if she kept her promise to Aurelius and gave him her love, she would have to marry him instead, and sorrow ever after.

"I thought it was impossible to get rid of the rocks," she murmured to herself tearfully. "It's against the process of nature for anything like that to happen. Otherwise I wouldn't have made any such promise to Aurelius. Can the rocks really be gone?"

Of course the rocks actually seemed to be gone.

At a loss to know what to do, she returned home sorrowfully, only to find that in her absence Arveragus had just arrived by boat from England and was waiting for her at the door, rejoicing at the thought of seeing her again and marrying her so soon. It did not occur to him that anything could have happened between them, because he knew that they were really in love with each other. He was amazed to see her so tearful. Tenderly he asked, "Dear love, what is the matter? Can't you tell me about it?"

But she only cried harder, until finally she was able to tell him the whole story of her rash promise and of how, so unexpectedly, she was now being asked to keep it. She looked at him expectantly, wondering what he would say. Would he blame her, or might he ask her to break her promise?

What Arveragus did, since he was a truly gentle man, was to take her in his arms and say, "My only love, you have made your promise, and I believe you must keep it. Even if it means losing you, I am unwilling to suggest anything else, for unless we keep our promises, life is not worth living. I shall bear the sorrow of losing you as best I can. Not keeping faith would be even worse." And although he could hardly bear doing it, he called some servants to take the weeping Dorigen to the garden.

Aurelius had started for the garden, too, but by chance the two of them happened to meet on the way. "Where are you going?" he asked her humbly.

"To the garden, to the garden!" she cried out, half mad with grief. "I am going to keep my promise, as my beloved Arveragus has told me to do!"

"What!" said Aurelius, "Arveragus, who loves you as much as I do, told you to do this, even though it means he must lose you? Do you mean that he is so gentle and good a man that he would rather lose you than tell you not to keep your promise?"

Dorigen told him he was right, and Aurelius stood lost in thought for a long time. He thought of all the trouble and sorrow that he had passed through in order to get Dorigen to do what he wanted. He thought how horrible it would be if he lost her now. But then he considered the upright and gentle decision of Arveragus, and he realized what he would have to do, for he was in many ways a good and gentle man himself.

Sighing deeply, Aurelius said, "Dorigen, this gentle deed of Arveragus, and your goodness, are too much for me. I must not take advantage of you in the way I had planned. Therefore, I hereby release you of the promise you made to me. I cannot break the great love there is between you and this

knight, and I now make another promise: I shall never require anything of you again, and I take my leave of you as the best and most loyal woman I have ever known. But please remember one thing. Just as a knight can do a gentle deed, so can a squire like me." And he went away.

Dorigen immediately returned to Arveragus, and they were married. They lived in the greatest bliss from that day forward, without a word of anger or jealousy, as people ought to do who have agreed of their own free will and love to obey each other. That is the end of their story.

But what of Aurelius? He cursed the day that he was born, because now he was a thousand pounds in debt to the magician and he did not have the money that he had unthinkingly promised because of his love. "I must keep my promise to give this learned man the money," he said to himself. "But it means I have to sell all my estate to do it, and then I shall be a beggar. I'll go to him and ask whether I can pay part of the gold now, and the rest a little at a time. That way I wouldn't have to sell my land. But if he won't consent, I'll have to pay it

all now. A promise is a promise; even if it means that I shall become a disgrace to all those who know me. If he demands all his money, I shall have to go away penniless from my dear land of Brittany."

So he went to the learned man at the university and asked him to accept the money a little at a time. This clerk looked at him and said very seriously, "Did I not keep my promise to you? Did I not remove the rocks from sight?"

"Yes, you did it faithfully and well," Aurelius answered.

"And did you not get the love of your lady?" the clerk asked.

"Ah, no, that I did not," said the squire.

The clerk asked him to tell why, and Aurelius told him the story you have just heard. "Arveragus did a gentle deed in telling his promised wife to keep her word, and Dorigen was obedient to him," said Aurelius. "They were so generous themselves that I had to be generous to them. I released Dorigen from her pledge."

The clerk thought a while and then answered, "Dear brother, each of you acted gently towards the other. You are a squire, and he is a knight. The Lord forbid that a clerk could not do a gentle deed, just as readily as you two. I hereby release you of your pledge to give me a thousand pounds, and I will not take a penny from you, now or hereafter. The hospitality you gave me at your house is enough for all that I have done," and having said that he bade Aurelius farewell.

So it happened that they all behaved in brotherly and gentle ways towards each other. But the question I, as a Franklin, should like to ask you is this: which one of them was the most generous? Tell me the answer to that, if you can. I don't know any more myself. My tale is at an end.

*Here Ends the Franklin's Tale*

# CHAUCER'S RIME OF SIR TOPAS
## The Prologue

WHEN THE FRANKLIN finished his tale, everyone was very thoughtful. There was a great deal of talk about what might be the best answer to his question. But no one could agree, and our Host was determined to get on with the tales. He turned briskly to me, and said: "What sort of a man are you? You look as if you were looking for rabbits—every time I look at you you're staring hard at the ground. Come closer, and cheer up!" He turned to the others and said, "Make room for him! Give him air! Why,

he's the same size around the middle I am! Can't you imagine this fine, slender figure of a man dancing with a fine lady? Now, sir," he said to me, "it's your turn. Do as others have done, and tell us a merry story."

"Host," said I, "please don't be angry with me: I just don't know any stories at all, except for an old rime."

"That's all right," said Harry Bailey kindly. He remarked to the others. "I expect we'll hear something really choice now, from the looks of him."

# The Rime of Sir Topas

*Fitt the First*

Listen, lords,
With all your might
And I shall tell
About a knight.

He always won
At every game;
Sir Topas was
This hero's name.

His face was white
As new-baked bread,
With rounded cheeks
Of flaming red.

He never soiled
His hands with toil,
So they were smooth
As olive oil.

He always wore
Expensive clothes
And had a most
Attractive nose.

Many a maiden
Young and fair
Loved his carrot-
Colored hair.

One day he rode
Out in the wood,
To find an elf-queen,
If he could.

For wild beasts such
As squirrel and deer
Brave Sir Topas
Felt no fear.

But when he came
To fairyland,
A giant stood there,
Axe in hand,

And told our hero,
"Go away."
Sir Topas thought
He wouldn't stay—

In fact, he thought
He'd better go,
Because he missed
His armor so.

Listen, lordings,
To my tale,
Merrier than the
Nightingale,

Of how Sir Topas
Came to town
To fetch his sword
And change his gown.

He called his men
And told them he
Would fight the giant,
Presently.

They brought him ale
And wine and mead,
And gingerbread,
On which to feed.

Then with his armor,
Shield and sword,
His gentle horse
He climbed aboard.

Now off into
The woods he lit,
And here, my lords,
There ends a fitt.

*Fitt the Second*

Now hold your tongues,
And I shall tell
Of all the wonders
That befell.

Men talk about
Such knights of old
As Lancelot
And Gawain bold,

But Sir Topas
Should take the prize—
He was so brave
And fair and wise.

Now forth he went
With fearless breast,
A lily flower
On his crest.

And since he was
A dauntless knight,
He never slept
Indoors at night.

And so he rode,
Till one fine day—

"No more of this, for heaven's sake!" cried our Host. "Your stupidity is making me so tired I swear my ears are aching with your rubbishy sing-song! To the devil with it! This is just doggerel!"

"Why so?" I asked, "Why won't you let me finish my tale, as you let the others, since it's the best I can do?"

"Look here," said he, "your dreadful riming isn't worth a bean. You're just wasting time. If you can't do better than that, you'd better try to tell us something in prose—something with some point to it."

"Gladly," said I. "I'll tell you a little thing in prose that I suppose you'll like. If you don't, then I give up—you're just too particular. This is a very virtuous, moral tale, and it has a very moral point to it. The Bible itself is hardly more instructive and moral than my merry little tale. I hope you'll all listen, and let me finish."

*Then Chaucer went on to tell his "little tale," which was indeed moral, but hardly little. The story was simple enough: Melibeus, a rich man, had enemies who came to his house one night, and robbed him and seriously injured his daughter, Sophy. He called all his friends to a council, to ask advice on whether he should take revenge. They all thought he should, except his wife, Prudence, who finally persuaded him not to. Prudence was just as great a talker as the Wife of Bath, and, like her, had no trouble ruling her husband. Her advice went on and on and on, as she quoted everyone Chaucer had ever heard of who was against fighting. The story turned out to be much the longest in the Canterbury Tales, and must have taken hours to tell.*

*But it certainly had a point. Oddly enough, the pilgrims loved it. When Chaucer finished, the Host exclaimed:*

"By the body of Saint Madrian, how I wish my wife could have heard that tale! Why, when I have to punish my boys, she comes running with great knobbed staffs and cries, 'Slay the dogs, every one!' And if a neighbor forgets to bow to my wife in church, she comes home and rants at me, and cries, 'Coward, avenge your wife! If you can't do it, you'd better take my apron and clean house and let me take your knife!' Night and day she goes on: 'Alas the day,' she says, 'that ever I was born to marry a milksop, a cowardly ape who lets himself be pushed around by everyone. You don't dare stand up for your wife's rights.' It is as much as my life is worth not to do what she wants, and fight anyone she imagines has snubbed her. But let's drop this subject."

# THE NUNS' PRIEST'S TALE
## The Prologue

OUR HOST then turned to the Nuns' Priest, and spoke boldly to him. "Come here, you priest, and tell us something to cheer us up. Be merry, even if you have to ride a broken-down old hag! What does it matter if your horse is old and skinny? If he'll carry you from place to place, that's all you should ask. Don't sulk!"

"Indeed, sir," answered the priest, "I should be very much to blame if I sulked." And immediately the good priest began to tell us a splendid story.

# Chanticleer and Pertelote

Once there was an elderly widow who lived in a very small cottage with her two daughters. They were very poor, and dined on bread and milk rather than roast meat and wine—an egg or a piece of bacon was a rare treat for these simple folk. They shared their cottage with three large pigs, three cows, and a sheep named Moll, so it was, as you can imagine, rather crowded—and not very clean. Outside, they had a

yard enclosed by a hedge of sticks and a deep ditch. In this yard they kept their prize possession, a cock whose name was Chanticleer.

In all that land there was no rooster that could compare with Chanticleer when it came to crowing; his voice was louder and clearer than the organ in the church. He was famous for always crowing right on time every single day, so that the people for miles around found him a more reliable guide to the time than any clock. Chanticleer's comb was redder than coral, with a beautiful jagged edge just like the towers of a castle. His bill was as black and shining as jet; his legs and toes were blue as azure, with nails whiter than a lily flower; and his feathers were the color of burnished gold.

This noble cock had seven hens in his flock, the most beautiful of whom was called the fair damsel Pertelote. Pertelote was gay, sweet, and courteous. She was so delightful in every way that she had completely won Chanticleer's heart from the time when they were barely a week old. Their great love was a continual joy to both of them, and it was really charming to hear those two singing together in perfect harmony at daybreak "My Love Is Like a Red, Red Rose"—for in those days, as I have heard, beasts and birds could speak and sing.

Now it happened that early one morning, as Chanticleer rested on his perch next to the fair Pertelote, he began to groan in his sleep like a man who is having a terrible nightmare. Pertelote was much alarmed, and shook him, saying, "Dear heart, what in the world is the matter? Why are you groaning so horribly?" He answered, "Please excuse me, madame. By heaven, I dreamed I was in such trouble just then that I'm still shaking with fear. May God help me to interpret my dream correctly, and keep me safe from danger! I dreamed that I was roaming around our yard, when I saw a beast who looked much like a dog, who wanted to grab me and kill me. His color was something between yellow and red, with black markings at the tips of the ears and tail. He had a thin snout, and glowing eyes. The very thought of him still makes me almost die of fear! That must be why I was groaning."

"Fie on you," cried Pertelote, "you coward! Alas, I certainly can't love a timid milksop! How dare you tell your love that anything can make you afraid! You ought to be ashamed of yourself. Don't you have a man's heart as well as a man's beard? Can it be possible that you should be afraid of a mere dream? There is nothing but nonsense in dreams—any child knows that. Dreams are caused by over-eating, fever, and illness of various kinds. This dream you had to-night must have been caused by indigestion. Certain feverish sorts of indigestion cause people to dream of fires with red flames, or red beasts about to bite them, just as chills cause dreams of black bears, black bulls, or even black devils. It's as simple as that. Don't you remember the words of Cato, the Roman who was so wise? He said, 'Put no faith in dreams.'

"Now, sir, take my advice: what you really need is a purge. I know what herbs will help to cure you, and you'd better not waste any time about it. If you're not careful, this could turn into a serious fever. I'll go and look for the herbs to make you a proper medicine—a nice brew of fumitory, castor beans, hellebore, caper berries, and ivy leaves should do the trick. But first, for a day or two, you should take doses of worms. Peck them right up from the ground, nice and fresh—and swallow them down. Cheer up, husband! And don't be afraid of any dream."

"Madame," said Chanticleer rather stiffly, "I thank you for your advice. But as far as Cato is concerned, he didn't know everything. When it comes to dreams, many wiser men than he wrote books proving just the opposite. It has been proved time and again that dreams predict future joys and sorrows —you don't have to take my word for it, it's a fact.

"One author," he went on, "tells the following true story. Once two travelers came into a town which was so full of people that they couldn't find a single cottage where there was room for both of them to spend the night. Therefore they had to part for the time being, one of them finding a bed in a private house, the other staying in the barn of an inn, sleeping with the oxen. During the night, the first man, lying in his bed, dreamed that his friend called to him, saying, 'Alas, tonight I shall be murdered in an ox's stall! Help me, dear friend, or I shall die! Come to me at once!'

"The dreamer jumped up in great terror, but when he was awake he just turned over again in his bed, deciding that it was nothing but a dream. Again he had the same dream, and still he paid no attention. Finally, he had a third dream, in which his friend came in, and said, 'I am dead now—see my bloody wounds. Get up early in the morning and go to the west gate of the town. There you will find a hay cart, in which my body is hidden. I was, of course, murdered for my money.' He went on to give all the details of his murder.

"Now mark well," Chanticleer continued, "this dream turned out to be true in every detail. In the morning the man whose sleep had been so disturbed by dreams went to the barn where his friend had been staying, and called for him. The innkeeper said, 'Sir, your friend has left. He went out at daybreak.' Remembering his dream, the man became very suspicious, and went immediately to the west gate of the town.

There he found just such a hay-cart as had been described in his dream. 'Vengeance!' he cried out, in a ringing voice. 'I demand justice for this crime! My friend was murdered last night, and his body is in this cart! Send for the officials of the town—alas, my friend lies here dead!' Immediately the people gathered around and turned over the cart—and there in the middle of the hay was the murdered man.

"It all goes to prove that murder will out, and also that dreams should be taken seriously. In the same book there is another story which proves the same thing," the cock went on. "Two men were about to go to sea, sailing to a distant city. They were, however, held up for many days, because the wind was from the wrong direction, and they could not start their journey until it changed. One evening the wind finally began to change. They were very thankful, and went to bed planning to set sail in the morning.

"But during the night one of the two had a marvelous dream. He thought a man stood by his bedside and told him not to start out that day, saying, 'If you sail tomorrow,

you will be drowned.' He woke up his friend and told him about the dream, and asked him to put off the journey for another day. But his friend just burst out laughing, and said scornfully, 'No dream could frighten *me* enough to change my plans. I don't care a straw for your dreams. It's too bad if you want to stay here and waste a favorable wind, but, as for me, I'm going.' So he left, and put out to sea. But out in the middle of the ocean the ship suddenly sprang a leak and sank, drowning all the men who were aboard.

"Therefore, sweet Pertelote," Chanticleer continued, "learn from these examples to respect dreams. Look in the Bible, at the story of Daniel, and you'll see if *he* thought dreams were nonsense. Read there about Joseph, also, and see whether dreams are not sometimes warnings of what is to happen. Didn't Pharaoh, the king of Egypt, find that his dreams had a real meaning? I could tell you many other examples from history. But now it is almost day, and I'd

better just say that I know very well this dream of mine means some sort of trouble.

"Furthermore, I set no store in purges: they're all poisonous, I know that quite well. I hate them one and all!

"Now that's enough about that. Let's turn to happier topics. Madame Pertelote, I know I'm lucky in at least one respect. When I look at your beautiful face—you do have such lovely scarlet-red circles around your eyes—it makes me forget about all my fears."

With these words Chanticleer flew down from the perch, since it was now day, and began to call his hens. Now he was not afraid of anything. He strutted around on his toes, looking as royal as a lion, and summoned all the hens with a loud "chuk!" whenever he found a grain of corn. Up and down the yard he roamed, attended by his hens like a prince with his court.

It was then early in the month of May. Chanticleer, walking along with his seven hens by his side, crowed happily, saying,

"Madame Pertelote, joy of my life, listen— how merrily the birds sing! And look at the flowers springing up everywhere. My heart is full of happiness." But alas, a terrible thing was about to happen to him. Happiness in this world is often all too soon gone; joy is followed by sorrow.

A sly fox, who had lived in the nearby woods for three years, had that very night burst through the hedges into the yard where noble Chanticleer and his hens spent their days. The fox hid quietly in a bed of cabbages all morning, waiting for a good time to attack Chanticleer. Oh, false murderer of a fox, lurking in your den! Oh Chanticleer, it was an evil morning when you flew into that yard! You were warned that this day was dangerous for you! But what must be, must be. The rooster most unfortunately took advice from his wife, and went into the yard even though he had been warned in a dream. Women's advice is all too often bad—it was taking a woman's advice that drove Adam from Paradise. (Or so they say—I don't mean to offend anyone! I certainly have nothing against women!)

While Pertelote and all her sisters lay in the sand, bathing themselves in the sunlight, Chanticleer sang more merrily than a mermaid. He happened to glance over at the cabbages, to look at a beautiful butterfly, and suddenly he saw the fox crouching there. He started up, breaking off his song in fright, and cried, "Cluk! Cluk!" He was filled with a natural desire to run away, although he had never seen a fox before in his life. But before he could get away, the fox said soothingly, "Dear sir, why are you going away? Surely you aren't afraid of me, your friend? I would never dream of hurting you—that's ridiculous. I didn't come to spy on your secrets, but only to listen to your singing. Truly, you have as merry a voice as an angel in heaven. You have more feeling for music than any musician I ever heard of. My lord your father (God bless his soul!) and your gentle mother have both been at

my house, to my great pleasure. Certainly, dear sir, nothing could please me more than to entertain you the same way.

"But speaking of singing—except for you, I never heard any man sing the way your father used to. He really sang from the heart. In order to make his voice stronger he was careful to close both his eyes, stand on his tip-toes, and stretch his neck out. He was so smart there was no one anywhere who could outdo him, either in singing or in knowledge. Now please sing for me, sir, and let's see: can you imitate your father?"

Chanticleer began to beat his wings back and forth with excitement, delighted with this flattery. He stood up high on his tip-toes, stretching his neck out, and, keeping his eyes closed, began to crow loudly. The fox jumped up at once, seized Chanticleer by the throat, and ran off towards the woods with the unhappy cock grasped firmly in his mouth.

The wails of the Trojan women, when the Greeks invaded their city and killed their king, were nothing in comparison to the outcry made by the seven hens when they saw Chanticleer carried off. Dame Pertelote shrieked louder than Caesar's wife did, when she saw Caesar murdered in the Forum. The cries of the hens were ten times stronger than those of the women of Rome, when Nero burned the city and murdered their husbands.

The poor widow and her two daughters heard the cries of the hens, and rushed out the door just in time to see the fox running across the field with the cock. They cried, "Help! Help! Woe, alas! Ha, the fox, the fox!" And after him they ran, with all the men of the village running behind them, sticks in hand. Coll, the dog, and Malkin, the kitchen maid, with her pot in her hand, ran after them—and the cows and the calf and even the pigs! The dogs barked, the

men and women shouted, and everyone ran like mad, yelling like devils. The geese were so frightened they flew up over the trees, and the noise was so hideous that even the bees came out of their hive. People brought brass trumpets, and horns made of wood or bone, and they blew up their cheeks and puffed and tooted until you would have thought the sky would have fallen down.

Hearing all this din, Chanticleer took courage and said to the fox, "Sir, if I were you, I'd turn to those people and say, 'Go on back home, you silly fools! A pox on the whole lot of you! You can't catch me, now that I'm at the edge of the forest. I have the cock, like it or not, and I'm going to eat him, too.'"

"I'll do it at once," said the fox; but the minute he had opened his mouth to speak, the cock got away and flew right up to the top of a high tree. When the fox saw that he had escaped, he said, "Alas, my friend Chanticleer, have I offended you? I must have frightened you when I took you up so suddenly, and carried you from the yard. I must apologize. But really, sir, I meant no harm. Come down, and I'll explain what I really had in mind—I swear that I'm telling you the truth."

"Oh no," answered Chanticleer. "I'm certainly not going to let you fool me more than once. Never again will your flattery persuade me to close my eyes while I sing. There is no excuse for a man who blinks just when he needs most to see."

"Well," said the fox gloomily, "there's just as little for a man who jabbers when he should hold his peace."

The Nuns' Priest concluded, "Those of you who think this is just a silly story about a fox, and a cock and a hen, pay attention to the moral. And may the Lord make us all good men."

*Here Ends the Nuns' Priest's Tale*

# THE PARDONER'S TALE
# The Prologue

"Sir nuns' priest," said our Host, "blessed be your jolly pate! That was a merry tale you told, and what a relief to hear something cheerful for a change! But what do the rest of you think of this priest? He's a regular Chanticleer himself, he looks so bold. He's got eyes like a hawk's. He's a good story-teller and a good man." Then, bubbling over with good spirits, he turned to the Pardoner to get him to tell a story.

The Pardoner was, perhaps, the most unattractive pilgrim of all. He had hair as yellow as wax, and it hung down and spread over his shoulders in straight locks like string. He wore no hood—he thought it was dashing and fashionable to ride bareheaded except for his cap. He had glaring eyes like a rabbit's, and a little voice like the bleating of a goat. None of us was so foolish as to believe that the old pillowcase in his satchel really was the Virgin Mary's veil, any more than we thought that the pig bones he had in a bag were the bones of saints, as he said they were. There was nothing trustworthy about this fellow at all. But he was a fine preacher, and sang the service in church so well that people were easily talked into buying his pardons. He loved money dearly, and he was very good at making it, so that he had every reason to sing both merrily and loud.

The Host said to this slimy-looking man, "You pretty fellow, you Pardoner, it's your turn—let's see if you can tell as merry a tale as the Nuns' Priest did."

"By Saint Runyan, it shall be done!" answered the Pardoner. "But first I want to get something to drink here at this tavern, to moisten my wit and make it grow."

At this there was a stir among the more well-bred pilgrims, who began to protest, "No, no! Don't let him tell us any drunken, coarse jests, we don't want to hear that sort of thing! If he'll tell us something moral,

so that we can learn something worthwhile, we'll listen gladly."

"I'll do that, too," said the Pardoner. "I'll try to think of something that will be highly moral while I drink my ale." And as he drank, he started: "Lords, when I preach in church I always preach upon one subject, and I always will. My text has always been the same: *Money is the root of all evil*. First, when I arrive in a new town, I show the priests and people my papers, which say that I come direct from Rome on church business. Then, to stir the people to devotion, and open their purses, I show them various things I carry around and sell as holy relics. To tell the truth, none of them is really worth a barley straw, but I can always persuade simple people to buy them anyway, just as I persuade them to pay me to pardon their sins. It's not so hard to talk people into parting with their money when you're as clever a speaker as I am. It's true that I myself love money better than anything in the world, but I can give such a fine sermon on the evils of money that the people are eager to give me their last penny. Although I'm hardly a moral man, I can tell a moral tale with the best of them. And now that I've finished my ale, if you'll hold your tongues I'll begin my tale."

# The Three Thieves

In Flanders some years ago there were three young men who lived a life of folly and wickedness. They spent their time drinking and gambling in taverns, playing dice night and day, throwing away money on dancing girls, and eating and drinking far more than they either needed or could possibly use. Their curses were so foul and bloodcurdling that it was really terrifying to hear them swear. Each of them laughed greatly at the other's sins. Needless to say, they could not get enough money by honest means to live such a life.

One day these three young men were sitting in a tavern drinking, although it was still quite early in the morning. While they were sitting there, they heard a bell tolling as a funeral procession passed by. One of them called to the serving boy and said, "Go out at once, and find out what corpse this is that is passing by—and make sure that you report his name correctly."

"Sir," said the boy, "there is no need to ask. I heard all about it before you came here, two hours ago. He was an old companion of yours. Last night he was here in

the tavern, sitting in his usual place, and very, very drunk, and suddenly he was slain. There came a thief called Death, who slays all the people in this land. He struck your friend in the heart with his spear—and went on his way. He has slain at least a thousand during this plague. Master, in case you meet him yourself, you had better beware of him. This is what my mother taught me; I don't know any more about it."

"By Saint Mary," said the tavern keeper, "the boy is right. This year Death has slain so many men, women, and children in a little village about a mile from here that I expect he must live there! Certainly it is best to be very careful and always be on the watch to avoid him."

"By heaven," said one of the drunken men, "is it then so dangerous to meet him? For myself, I vow I shall seek him in every highway and byway. Listen, comrades, we three should be in this together. Let each of us hold up his hand and swear to be a brother to the others, and help them in all things, and then we will slay this false traitor Death. He, that slays so many others, shall himself be slain before nightfall!"

The others agreed, and all three swore to live and die together as brothers. Up they jumped in their drunken rage and started towards the village which the tavern keeper had mentioned. By many a grim and bloody oath they vowed that Death would die if they could catch him.

When they had gone not quite half a mile, they met a wretched-looking old man. He greeted them politely and meekly, and said, "God protect you, my lords."

The proudest of the three answered with a sneer, "Well, fellow, you're certainly a sorry sight! Why are you all wrapped up, except for your face? Why do you go on living so long, as old as you are?"

The old man looked him full in the face, and said quietly, "Why? Because I could not find a man anywhere, even if I walked from here to India, who would exchange his youth for my old age. Therefore I must keep my age as long as it is God's will. Nor will Death take my life. So I must walk like a restless captive. On the ground, which is my mother's gate, I knock with my staff and say, 'Dear mother, let me in! Look how I am fading away, flesh, and blood, and breath. Alas, when shall my bones be at rest?' But still she will not grant my wish, and that is why my face is pale and withered.

"But, sirs, it is not courteous of you to speak so rudely to an old man. Let me give you some advice: Do not harm an old man now any more than you wish men to harm you when you are old—if you live to be the same age. Now God be with you, wherever you go; I must be on my way."

"Oh no you don't, you old rogue," said another of the three. "By Saint John, you're not getting away from us that easily. You spoke just now of that traitor Death, who kills all our friends in this country. Since you seem to be his spy, tell us where he is, or we'll make you pay dearly for it! False thief, we know you're on his side, planning to slay us young folk!"

"Sirs," said the old man, "if you are so eager to find Death, turn up this crooked path. I left him there in the wood, under a tree, and there he shall stay. I assure you your boasts won't make him hide. Do you see that oak? You'll find him right there. May God save you, and may He help you to mend your ways."

None of them paid any further attention to the old man, for at once they all ran to the tree he had pointed out. But there, to their enormous delight and astonishment, they saw a huge pile of shining gold coins— there seemed to be about eight bushels of them. They forgot all about looking for Death, since each of them was overjoyed at the dazzling sight of the bright gold. They sat down to gaze at this precious pile, and the worst of the three was the first to speak. "Brothers," said he, "pay careful attention to what I say. My wits are sharp, even if I usually seem to use them only in joke. Fortune has given us this treasure so that we can live our lives in jollity and games. It came lightly, and it is right that we should spend it lightly. Who would have thought that we should have such luck today? But the gold must be carried home from this place to my house—or yours— before we can really enjoy it. However, we certainly can't do it by day, for then people would say that we were bold thieves and hang us for taking our own treasure. It must be carried away by night, as slyly and secretly as possible. So I suggest that we draw lots, and he whose lot it is shall immediately run to the town and bring us all bread and wine. The other two will keep guard over the treasure while he is gone. Then when it is night, we'll take the treasure to whatever place we all agree is best. Here, brothers—draw lots."

They drew lots, and the lot fell to the youngest. He started out towards the town at once. As soon as he had gone, the one who had suggested the plan turned to the other, and said, "You know that you are my sworn brother. Now I'm going to tell you something for your own good. You know well that our comrade is gone, and here we have a great deal of gold which is to be divided among the three of us. However, if I can manage things so that it will only be divided among the two of us, won't I be doing a favor for you?"

The other answered, "I don't know how that can be done. He knows that we have the gold. What shall we do? What can we say to him?"

"If you'll swear to secrecy," said the first villain, "I'll tell you in a few words what we can do."

"I swear it," said the other. "I wouldn't dream of betraying you."

"Now then," said the first, "you know well that we are two, and two of us are bound to be stronger than one. As soon as he comes back and sits down, you get up as if you wanted to wrestle with him in fun. While you struggle with him, as if in play, I'll stab him in the side and back. At the same time, you draw your own dagger and do likewise. Then, dear friend, all this gold shall be divided between you and me. We two can have everything we desire, and play at dice to our hearts' content."

And so the two villains agreed between themselves to slay the third in this manner. Meanwhile, the youngest of the three, as he went to the town, thought a good deal about the beauty of the bright gold coins. "Lord," he said to himself, "if only I could have all this treasure to myself alone, there wouldn't be a man in the world who could live more merrily than I." And it wasn't long before it came into his mind that he could buy poison, in order to kill both his companions and get all the gold for himself.

Walking at a fast pace, he wasted no time. He went at once to a druggist in the town and asked him for some poison to kill the rats in his barn, as well as a skunk which, he said, was carrying off all his chickens. The druggist was sympathetic, and assured him, "I'll give you something that no creature alive can eat or drink without losing his life. Even if he has a bit of it as small as a grain of wheat, this poison is so strong and deadly, he shall die in less time than it takes to walk a mile."

The villain was well pleased with this recommendation and bought the poison. He took the box in his hand and went on to a shop in the next street. There he bought three bottles of wine, and in two of them he poured his poison. The third he kept pure for himself, knowing he would need it to give him the strength to work all night carrying away all the gold.

When he returned to his comrades they killed him in the manner that they had planned. When that was done, one of them said, "Now let's sit and drink and be merry; we'll bury his body later." And as he spoke he happened to pick up one of the poisoned bottles, and drank from it, and gave his comrade a drink from it also. And so they were both poisoned.

Thus were the two murderers slain, and the false poisoner as well. They had found Death under the oak tree, although they had not recognized him in the pile of gold.

*Here Ends the Pardoner's Tale*

"Now, good men," said the Pardoner, "may God pardon all your sins, and keep you from the sin of avarice, and all the evils

which come from the love of money." And, since he usually told such stories as part of a sermon, he went on to finish the sermon in his usual way: "I have the power to grant you all pardons, if you'll offer me gold or silver. Step up, you wives, and offer up your fine woolens, and I'll put your name in my book! Any of you who want pardons, come forth, and I'll give them to you, at a price. Or if you prefer, I'll give you pardons as we go, a new one at the end of each mile, provided you pay me every time! Aren't you lucky to have me, a real Pardoner, with you on this trip? Who knows? Maybe one of you will fall off your horse and break your neck. You never can tell what's going to happen on the road, and a comprehensive pardon is the best insurance to cover such risks. I think the Host

had better step up first, since he looks like a terrible sinner. Come forth, sir Host, and make your offering, and I'll let you kiss my relics for only a shilling!"

"Not on your life!" cried the Host. "You rascal, you'd be likely to make me kiss the rottenest egg you could find, and swear it was the relic of a saint!"

The Pardoner was speechless with anger, and the Host began to curse the Pardoner with the worst insults he could think of, to the great amusement of some of the pilgrims, but the Knight stepped between them, and said, "No more of this; you have both said enough! Sir Pardoner, be merry and pleasant; and you, sir Host, whom I love, I pray you embrace the Pardoner. Let us all ride on together as good friends."

So they embraced and jogged on.

# THE CANON'S YEOMAN'S TALE
## The Prologue

WE RODE ON five miles and more without anyone's telling a story. Then, at the town of Boughton-under-Blean, two men overtook us, riding very fast. One of them, who seemed to be the master, had on a black cloak and hood under which he wore a loose white clerical gown. After wondering about it for a while, I decided that he must be the kind of priest called a canon. His dapple gray horse was sweating greatly: it must have been galloping steadily for at least three miles, and it was flecked all over with foam. His yeoman-servant had been galloping his horse, too, which was so sweated and exhausted that it could hardly walk.

The canon's bag for his belongings lay on the crupper of his horse. It was folded in two, as though there weren't much inside. His hat hung down by a lace in back of his head: he had been galloping too fast to keep it on, but he had his hood up over his head, and under it he had put a large burdock leaf to absorb his perspiration and to keep him cooler. He was sweating as much as his horse, so that his face was all red and his forehead dripped like a distilling apparatus over a fire.

As soon as he caught up with us, he called out, "God save all this jolly company! I have been galloping so fast on account of you. I wanted to catch up with you and get a bit of the fun." His yeoman was full of polite speeches, too. "This morning," he said, "I saw you leaving the inn, and I told my master here. He particularly wants to ride in your company because he loves to have a lively time on a trip."

Our Host was curious about this strange pair, and as a good innkeeper he knew that you can find out more from the servant than from the master. So he spoke privately to the servant: "Friend," he said, "God reward you for having told your master about us! He seems to be a prudent man; at least, I'm willing to take that part of it on faith. And I'm willing to bet he's a cheerful man, too, eh? Could he tell a story or two, do you think, to cheer us all up?"

"Who? My master?" replied the servant. "Of course he can. He knows plenty about that kind of thing. But there's something else about him, too, that's a lot more important. You would be simply amazed at the marvelous things he can do. He has taken on himself many a great task that no one here could accomplish unless my master told him how to. No matter how friendly and familiar he seems as he rides among you, he really is very important. I'm willing to bet everything I have that you'd try hard to be friendly to him if you knew who he was. Let me tell you, he's a remarkable man."

Our Host pricked up his ears. "Well," he said, "he must be a learned man, or something like that, isn't he? Just what kind of a person is he, after all?"

"Oh, he's much more than a learned man," replied the servant quickly. "Let me tell you, in just a few words, something about the kind of thing he can do. I help him, but I'm not the man he is, so I can't tell you exactly how he does it. But as an example of what he is capable of doing, let me tell you this—do you see this ground we're riding on? Well, my master could take all the ground from here until we come to Canterbury, and turn it upside-down and then pave it all with silver and gold!"

"Well, well, well," said the Host, opening his eyes wide and putting one finger beside his nose. "There's something peculiar about all this that I don't understand. If your master knows so much that people ought to respect him, why isn't he a little bit more careful about the way he looks? His gown certainly isn't good enough for a man like him, and besides, it's all dirty and torn. Why is your lord so badly dressed if he has the power that you say he has? Tell me that!"

"You're asking me why?" said the yeoman. "How should I know?" His mood seemed to change, and his face became bitter. The Host was beginning to get at the truth. "I'll tell you what I think," the servant whispered, "if you'll promise not to tell. I think my master is too smart for his own good. Wise men say that you can have too much cleverness, and then it becomes a vice. That's what's wrong with my master, and I am very sorry for it. But I can't tell you any more."

"Never mind," said the Host heartily. "It doesn't make any difference what the reason is. But since you know so much about the great knowledge of your master, tell me if you can, where do you live?"

"On the outskirts of a town," replied the servant bitterly, "lurking around corners and blind alleys where thieves hide away, and other people who are afraid to show themselves. That's the way we are, to tell the truth." The servant had finally given up all pretense of cheerfulness.

"Well, now," said Harry Bailey, "let me ask you something else. Why is your face such a peculiar color?"

"Lord!" said the Yeoman. "How I hate that color! It comes from my continual blowing in the fire, when my master and I are making our chemical experiments to turn various substances into gold. That is what all the other alchemists do, and that is what we really are—alchemists. I don't have any time for looking at myself in a mirror. I labor away painfully all the time

to learn how to make the right experiment. We flounder on with our experiments, peering into the fire continually, but in spite of everything we never get our desire, because the experiment never turns out right. Not only that, but we're always fooling other people, too. We borrow gold—a pound or two, or maybe ten or twelve or a lot more—and we make them think that at the least we can make two pounds for every one. It's all false, but we keep on hoping and groping for the right method. But the true knowledge is so far ahead of us that we'll never reach it; it keeps retreating before us. Our art of alchemy will make beggars of us in the end."

While the yeoman was talking thus mournfully, his master the canon drew near and overheard everything that was said, for he was suspicious of everybody, as many people are who deceive others. He spoke up suddenly and sharply: "Hold your peace. Another word, and you'll pay dearly for it. You're slandering me and revealing things that should be kept secret!"

"Oh, no, you don't!" exclaimed Harry Bailey. "Yeoman, go on and tell us more. Don't pay any attention to his threats!"

"In good faith, I don't pay much attention to them," said the yeoman, shrugging his shoulders.

When the canon saw that there was no way of keeping his servant from telling the truth about him, he was bitterly ashamed. He put spurs to his horse and galloped away from the company so quickly that he was soon out of sight.

"Aha!" muttered the servant, "so that's the way it is! Now the fat's in the fire, I might as well tell you all I know. Since he's stolen away from me, may the devil accompany him! I'll never go near him again for anything. He was the one who first started me on the experiments of alchemy, and may he have sorrow and shame for it! Alchemy has ruined me, but for all my pains and grief, for all my labor and misfortunes, I could never let it alone. I wish to heaven that I had the wit to tell you all about it, but, anyway, I'll tell you part. Since my master is gone, I'll tell you everything I know. We were going to trick you into giving money for our experiments, but instead of that I'm going to tell you such a story about an alchemist that you'll never listen to another man who offers to change anything into gold."

The servant was so bitter about what had happened to him that he tried to tell us some of the secrets of alchemy even before he began his story. This was just as well, because his explanations helped us to understand the story itself.

# The False Alchemist

I'm an ignorant man, so that I can't begin to tell you how complicated and discouraging the whole art of alchemy is. One of the things we always do is to try to turn quicksilver, or mercury, into real silver. We heat up all kinds of chemicals in a crucible, or pot, to try to bring about this transformation. Everything has to be measured and weighed very carefully, but after we're finished with the whole long process, and with our orpiment, and our mercury, and our litharge ground on the porphyry slab, and our agrimony, and our valerian, and our moonwort, and whatever else costs a lot of money, then we're just where we were before, and what we have isn't worth an onion. I could give you enough strange names of chemicals to raise a devil by magic from hell, but what we can't raise is the philosopher's stone, called the elixir, that turns everything into silver or gold. If we had it, we'd be happy enough. But we never get it, even though we spend huge amounts of money searching for it.

Still, we keep on trying our experiments. Sometimes the pot breaks and everything

blows up or falls down. Then every alchemist there blames the others. "The fire was laid wrong," one of them says. "No! the fire was *blown* wrong," someone else shouts (This always scares me, because I blow the fire). "The chemicals weren't mixed right!" yells somebody else. "That's nonsense; it's because you didn't use beech-wood to make the fire!" another one pipes up. Then they sweep up all the mess of wasted chemicals on the floor and put them through a sieve to see what they can save. Everybody cheers up and they decide to start all over again. "Who knows?" somebody says hopefully. "Maybe there was a crack in the pot."

Mostly it's the alchemists who are cracked. Even if they had nothing but a sheet for night and a cloak without lining for day, they'd sell them and spend the money on new chemicals. You can always tell alchemists by their sulphur smell and by their clothes. They smell as bad as a goat, and you can catch a whiff of them a mile off. They always wear threadbare clothes, but if you ask an alchemist why he dresses so poorly, he'll whisper in your ear that if people really knew how wealthy he'd made himself, they'd kill him out of envy for his great knowledge! The wisest-sounding alchemist always turns out to be a fool, and, what's more, the one who seems most honest is a thief. Just listen to my story.

There was a canon among us alchemists who was so false and dishonest that he would spoil a whole town, even if it was as big as Nineveh, Rome, Alexandria, Troy, and three others all rolled up into one. But he was so skilled at telling lies and talking fast that he could pull the wool over anyone's eyes.

One day this false canon came to see a priest who lived in a rented room in London. This priest was so pleasant and helpful to his landlady that she would never let him pay for his board, or even for his clothing, no matter how well he dressed. Even better, she gave him plenty of money to spend. The canon said to the priest, "Lend me a gold piece for just three days, and if I don't pay you back by then, hang me by the neck!" The priest lent it to him willingly, and the canon was profuse in his thanks. He brought back the money as he had promised on the third day, so that the priest said, "It certainly wouldn't bother me at all to lend a man even more money when he is so faithful to his promise. I can't say 'No' to a man like that."

"Good heavens," replied the canon, "did you think I wouldn't keep my promise? That would certainly be a novelty. Keeping promises is something that I've always done and always will do until I go down into my grave. Believe me as completely as you believe your Bible: no man has ever come off badly from lending me gold or silver, and I have never in my life told a lie."

"Good for you," said the priest.

"And now," continued the canon, "since you have been so kind to me, I am going to tell you a secret that may help to pay you back. I'm going to show you what I can accomplish by alchemy. Watch carefully, and you will see with your own eyes that I shall do something marvelous before I leave this room."

"Is that so?" said the priest. "Well! Please show it to me. I'm very anxious to see it."

"Just as you wish, sir; I said I would keep my word and I always do," said the accommodating canon.

You see how easily and craftily this canon wound himself into the unsuspecting priest's good graces. I blush to think how wily a fox this alchemist was—ten times worse than my master. And you know I can't blush very easily, because the fumes from all those chemicals have ruined my natural complexion.

Now listen to what he did next: "Sir Priest," he said, "send your servant out to buy two or three ounces of quicksilver." The priest did so, and when the quicksilver came, the canon told the servant to prepare a fire with a bed of glowing wood-coals. Then the canon produced a crucible from the bosom of his cassock, where he had been

keeping it, and said to the priest, "Take this crucible and put an ounce of quicksilver into it—that's right. Now you are beginning to become an alchemist. There are very few people who are allowed to see this much of my art. You will see me change this quicksilver into real silver right before your eyes. It will be as pure as any silver coin in your purse. I have a powder here that is the secret of all my power; it cost me many a pound. Send your servant out of the room and shut the door, so that we shall be absolutely private when we work this miracle of alchemy."

The priest did so, and then put the crucible upon the fire and blew on the coals vigorously, as the canon told him. The canon threw his powder into the crucible—I don't know what it was made of—perhaps chalk, or ground glass, or something else not worth a bean—it was just to fool the priest. Then the canon said, "Just to prove how much I like you, I'm going to let you do all the rest of this with your own hands. That way, you'll be sure that there's no trickery involved."

"Thank you very much," said the happy priest, and began piling up red-hot coals all around and over the crucible as the canon told him to do. But while he was busy doing this, that scoundrel the canon took a charred and half-burned coal from his sleeve and kept it hidden in his hand. Before he had come to the priest's room he had hollowed out part of this coal and put an ounce of silver inside; then he had stopped up the hole with wax.

"Friend," said the canon suddenly and unexpectedly, "you're not piling up those coals the way they ought to be. Let me handle it for just a minute. I see you've made yourself all hot, and I'm sorry for you. Here, take this towel and dry off your face." While the priest had his face covered with the towel, the canon swiftly put the hollowed-out coal at the top of the heap of other coals, right over the opening in the crucible. Then he blew hard on the coals until the hollowed-out one was hot enough to start flaming like the others.

"Now!" said the canon, "Let's have something to drink. Everything will be finished in a little while, and we might as well make merry while we wait." While they were drinking, the canon's hollow coal burned up and all the silver fell down into the crucible. When the canon knew that everything was ready, he said to the priest, "I know you don't have any mold for silver here. Let's go out and buy a large piece of chalk stone. I'll hollow it out to the shape of an ingot of silver. We'll have to have a large pan of water, too, and then you'll see.

But just so you'll be sure there is no foul play, I'll come out with you to fetch these things, and we can lock the door behind us." They did all this, the priest holding onto the key all the while.

When they got back to the room, the canon secretly took a little rod of silver from his sleeve; it weighed an ounce— exactly the same weight that he had put into his hollow coal. He made the hollow in the chalk stone exactly the same size as the rod, so that it would hold an ounce and no more. He put the rod away again in his sleeve, where he could get at it later. Finally, he took the crucible from the fire, poured what was melted in it into the mold in the chalk stone, and happily put the whole thing in the bowl of water to cool and become solid. The pure silver stayed in the

mold, but the quicksilver, being lighter, rose to the top and rolled away.

"Put your hand in the water and grope around, Sir Priest," said the canon heartily. "You're bound to find silver there! What else could it be? Silver's silver." The priest doubtfully stuck his hand into the bowl, and pulled out a rod of pure silver.

He was as happy as a bird. "The blessings of heaven light on your head, Sir Canon," he said, "I'm your man forever if you teach me this noble craft!"

But the canon wasn't ready yet. "Let's try once more," he said soberly, "so that you can watch carefully and become an expert in the art. Take another ounce of quicksilver and do the same thing with it that you did before."

This time the priest worked very hard and fast. While he was blowing himself red in the face to make the fire hot, the canon threw in his powder and then took a stick that he had brought along with him and started stirring the coals. He said this would make them burn better. But before he had come to fool the priest, he had hollowed out the stick in the same way he had hollowed out his coal, and had filled the end of the stick with an ounce of silver held in with a plug of wax, just as he had done before. As he stirred, the wax melted and the silver fell down into the crucible. Then the priest poured the melted metal from the crucible into the chalk mold and put the mold into the pan of water. Naturally he ended up with another pretty bar of silver.

By this time the priest was ready to turn himself over, body and soul, to the canon, if he could only learn how to go on making silver. But the canon wanted to make sure his man was on the hook. "Is there any copper here?" he asked. There wasn't any, but the priest rushed out to buy some. When he had returned with it to the room, the canon weighed out exactly an ounce and put it into the crucible. They went through the whole business again, but this time the canon did not slip anything into the fire. When the molten metal had been poured into the mold and put into the pan, the canon started groping around in the water, as though he wanted to find what was there. But while he was groping, he slipped the silver rod from his sleeve into the bottom of the pan and slyly hid the copper one. Then he said gleefully to the priest, slapping him on the back as he did so, "Now you help me the way I helped you! Put your hand in the water and see what you find." The priest, of course, pulled out the silver.

"Now," said the canon, "let's take these three rods to a goldsmith, so that he can tell

us whether they really are silver. It would be terrible if they turned out to be something else, but let's get an expert to tell us."

This they did. The goldsmith tried out the rods with his fire and his hammer, and assured the priest and the canon that the silver was as pure as it could be made.

No nightingale was ever more anxious to sing, and no knight was ever more anxious to do a deed that would bring him into his lady's grace, than the priest was to persuade the canon to give him the recipe for the powder that worked this miracle. "For holy charity," he cried out, grabbing the canon by the arm, "tell me how much money you want for the secret of the powder! I'm ready to give anything for it." And so he was.

"Trust me well," answered the canon, "it's terribly expensive. There's only one man in England besides me who knows how to make it, and he's a friar."

"I don't care how much it costs!" shouted the priest frantically. "Just tell me, please!"

"Well," said the canon, "it's expensive; I've already told you that. To be absolutely frank, I can't give it to you for less than five hundred pounds. And if you hadn't been so generous with me before, and if we weren't such good friends, I'd have to charge you a great deal more."

The priest promptly rushed out, got together five hundred pounds, and gave them to the canon. Then the canon gave him a recipe—I don't know what was in it, but it wasn't worth a butterfly. The canon said solemnly, "Sir Priest, you must remember that I'm not interested in fame. If people in general knew that I have such knowledge, I shouldn't be alive a day. They would kill me out of envy for this knowledge. So please keep this precious craft secret. Only you and I should know of it."

"Absolutely!" said the priest. "You can trust me. I'd rather lose everything than have anything bad happen to you."

"Thank you tremendously," answered the canon, pressing the priest's hand. "For the sake of your good will and generosity, I heartily wish that everything turns out all right. Now farewell! Goodbye! So long!"

Off the canon went, and the priest never saw him again. Shortly afterward, the priest tried out the recipe, and of course you know what happened—nothing.

You see what I mean when I say it's best to keep away from alchemy. I don't know whether anyone will ever find the philosopher's stone or elixir, which turns any substance into gold. But I do know that we shouldn't meddle with it, for it is one of nature's secrets. All the great philosophers have known this. A disciple of the philosopher Plato once asked him the name of this secret stone. Plato answered, "It is called Titanos." "What is Titanos?" asked the disciple. "Titanos is Magnasia," replied Plato. "Yes, sir," said the disciple, "but what kind of a thing is Magnasia?" "Magnasia is a liquid made of four elements," Plato assured him. "Then tell me the recipe for it," implored the disciple. "That I will not do," Plato said. "All philosophers have taken an oath not to reveal the secret, because it is so dear to the Lord of the universe. Only He knows when it is right to inspire a man with the secret, and when it is right to deny another man the privilege."

So I come to the end of my story in this way: We should let the philosopher's stone alone. Since God will reveal it only of His own free will and grace, it is working against His will to try to change His creation to gold for our own purposes. My tale is ended. May every honest man find the cure for his sorrow!

*Here Ends the Canon's Yeoman's Tale*

# THE MANCIPLE'S TALE
## The Prologue

As we passed the little town called Bob-Up-and-Down, our Host turned to the rest of us and said, "Can't anyone here wake up our comrade the Cook back there? He's about to fall off his horse! Make him come forward and tell a tale, even if it isn't worth a bundle of hay. Wake up, Cook! What's the matter with you, sleeping in the daytime? Did the fleas keep you awake all night, or have you been drinking so much wine that you can't hold up your head?"

The Cook, who was looking terribly pale, said sleepily, "Bless my soul! I don't know why, but I'd rather sleep than have the best gallon of wine in London!"

"Well," said the Manciple, "if our Host and this company will permit, it seems to me that you ought to be excused from telling your tale. Your face is very pale and your eyes are fixed—you certainly look perfectly awful. You're drunk, and it isn't a pretty sight."

The Cook was furious at the Manciple's remarks, and he tried to answer, but he could only manage to nod his head violently up and down. This immediately made him fall off his horse—and there on the ground he lay, until some of us picked him up. He should have stayed home in the first place, and tended to his ladles. There was "Hi!" and "Ho!" and much pulling and hauling, as we tried to get the dead weight of him back on his horse, as though he were a sack of wheat.

Then our Host turned to the Manciple, saying, "I'm afraid wine has got the better of this man, so that he could hardly be expected to tell a tale well. He'd better concentrate on trying to stay on his horse. If he falls off again, we shall have no end of trouble trying to put the pieces back together. You tell a tale—I give up as far as he is concerned. But you'd better watch out, Manciple; you spoke too sharply to him, and he's apt to hold a grudge against you forever."

"I certainly don't want to quarrel with him," said the Manciple. "I was only joking. Here, I have a flask of wine of my own, and I should be delighted if the Cook would have a drink from it."

The Cook accepted the drink all too eagerly, and thanked the Manciple, so that they were friends again. Our Host laughed heartily, and said, "All right, Manciple—tell your tale."

# How the Crow Became Black

When the god Apollo lived here on the earth among men, as many old books tell, he was the finest young man in all the world, and the very best archer. He performed many brave deeds with his bow, including killing dragons. He could play every musical instrument, his singing was the most beautiful ever heard, and he was the most handsome man in the world. Never since the world began was there a more honorable, worthy person.

Apollo had a crow in a cage as a pet in his home, and he fed and cared for it tenderly. This crow, which was white as any swan, he had taught to speak. The crow could also sing a thousand times better than any other bird. In all the world no nightingale could sing anywhere near so merrily and sweetly as this crow could.

Apollo also had a sweetheart, a lady whom he loved more than his life. Day after day he did everything he could to please and honor her, and there was little he could not do for her because he was a god. However, to tell the truth, he had one sad fault as a lover: He was terribly jealous, and apt to be most unreasonable in his jealousy. He was a little ashamed of this, for he wasn't really ever worried about losing her; he knew he did everything she could ask of him, and he knew also that he was a much better man than any other.

But, unfortunately, some people just aren't trustworthy, and by nature are unable to appreciate what they are given. You may give a cat milk and fresh meat, and a silken cushion to sleep on, but the minute the cat sees a mouse go by the wall she forgets all about the milk and the meat and everything else in her desire to get the mouse. So it was

with Apollo's beloved, for she began, behind his back, to encourage another man, a poor fellow indeed in comparison with the young god. Finally, one day when this man was a guest in Apollo's home, the lady met him alone in a room where there were no other people, and allowed him to court her there under Apollo's own roof. But the crow was in his cage, and he saw all that went on, although he did not say a word.

The next day, when Apollo stopped to enjoy the company of his pet, the bird began to sigh, and to sing a mournful, off-key song.

"Why, bird!" said Apollo. "What on earth are you singing? Haven't you always sung so merrily that it refreshed my heart to hear you? What sort of a song is this?"

"Ah, master," said the bird, "if you had seen what I have seen you would not be able to sing merrily either. In spite of your nobility, your brave deeds, and your gentleness, and in spite of all you have done for her, your lady has betrayed you and is deserting you for a wretch who is not worth a gnat compared to you. I saw it myself."

The crow told him every detail of their conversation, so that his master could not help believing him. Apollo thought his heart would break for sorrow. In his anger he ran and fetched his bow and shot an arrow through his sweetheart's breast.

But when he saw what he had done—that he had killed his beloved—his sorrow was even greater. He went at once and broke all his musical instruments, harps and lutes and everything else, and also his bow and arrows. After that he went back and spoke to the crow. "Traitor," he said, "it is your vile tongue that has brought me to this. Alas, that ever I was born! Oh, my dear

lady, so lovely and gentle! You are dead, and I fear you were guiltless! Oh, rash hand, to do such a foul deed! How could I have been so carried away with anger and despair, to give way to low suspicion! As for you, you false thief of a crow, I'll get even with you for your tale-telling. You used to sing like a nightingale, but now your song shall be gone forever, and your beautiful white feathers as well. Just as men who mourn for the dead must wear black, so your clothes, which are your feathers, shall forever be black. And you and your children shall not make any sweet noises, but only rough cries, all because you have caused the death of my love.

He ran up to the crow, replaced all his white feathers with black ones, and threw him out of the house. Ever since then all crows have worn the mournful color of black, in memory of this crow and how he caused the death of Apollo's beloved.

My lords, take warning from this tale never to tell a man bad news as this crow did, for certainly he will hate you for it. Guard your tongue, and remember the story of the crow.

*Here Ends the Manciple's Tale*

"And never tell a cook, or anyone else, that he has made a fool of himself with drink! Remember the crow, and you'll never make an enemy," added the Host.

# THE MAN OF LAW'S TALE
## The Prologue

WHEN THE MANCIPLE had finished his tale, our Host glanced up at the sun and saw that the day was almost over. He pulled his horse about suddenly and addressed all the pilgrims. "My lords, the day is drawing on, and we must try not to waste what little time is left. Sir Man of Law, you seem like a man who never wastes a minute. Tell us a tale now, as you have agreed. You have consented, of your own free will and desire, to let me be the judge in this case and have jurisdiction over you. It is agreed and stipulated by your contract that you should tell a tale. Now do your duty."

"Host," answered the Man of Law, in his most polite courtroom manner, "I have duly sworn it, and I'll keep my contract. A promise is as binding as a debt; and as I pay my debts, I desire to keep my promises. Whatever law a man expects his fellows to keep, he must keep himself."

The Lawyer and the Host bowed to each other, and the Man of Law proceeded to tell his tale.

# The Calamities of Constance

Long ago, in the land of Syria, there lived a company of wealthy merchants who traded their spices and rich fabrics all over the world. Their merchandise was so low in price and so high in quality that other merchants everywhere were delighted to do business with them. It happened once that several of these merchants decided to make a trip to Rome, both for pleasure and for business. While they were in that great city, they were naturally eager to see all the sights and hear all the news, and they listened eagerly to all that the Romans around them said.

They noticed that one name seemed to be mentioned more often than any other, and this was the name of a princess called Constance, who was the daughter of the Roman

emperor. Their curiosity was aroused by the constant praises they heard of this lady, of whom it was said that she was not only the most beautiful lady in the world, but also the best and most virtuous. The people of Rome so admired Constance that her name was on every tongue. When the Syrian merchants asked why this was, they were apt to get an answer such as this: "Our emperor has a daughter who deserves to be queen of all Europe. She has beauty without pride; youth without foolishness; she is the mirror of all courtesy."

Naturally, the merchants did not wish to leave Rome without getting a glimpse of this princess, and, when they had stocked their ships and all was ready for the voyage home, they paid a call at the emperor's court and beheld the princess for themselves. They could easily see that all that had been said in her praise was absolutely true.

When the merchants returned home to Syria, the sultan who ruled that country invited them to come to a banquet at his palace. This was his usual custom, for in this way he was not only entertained, but

also learned much about what was going on in other countries.

The merchants were royally entertained with course after course of the most delectable food that could be obtained, served on precious dishes of gold and silver by the most beautiful dancing girls the sultan could find. After dinner the sultan asked them many questions about what they had learned on their travels. Among other tidings, the merchants naturally told him about the princess Constance, praising her goodness and beauty so greatly that the sultan decided there and then that he wanted to have this lovely princess as his wife.

The sultan called his councilors together and told them that he was determined to marry Constance, and no other. He charged them to find a way in which he could bring this about. His councilors shook their heads and became very grave. They knew this might mean serious difficulties, because Syria and Rome were so distant from each other and had such entirely different customs and religions, that it seemed hardly possible the emperor would consent to such a marriage.

Finally one of the oldest and most respected of the councilors stepped forward, and, speaking for the entire group, said, "Sire, we do not think that this can be. No Christian prince would wish to marry his child to a Moslem." But the sultan answered, "Rather than lose Constance, I will make myself a Christian. Now cease your arguments, and arrange the marriage."

Ambassadors were sent to Rome, and finally an agreement was reached. According to the treaties signed on both sides, the sultan was to have Constance for his wife provided that he would himself become a Christian. The agreement also required that all the nobles of the sultan's court must be christened, too.

When the treaty had been signed, the emperor made all proper preparations for his daughter to go to Syria with a great escort of knights and ladies. He sent out a proclamation all through the land asking his people to pray for the success of the marriage and for a safe voyage for the bride.

Soon the day came when Constance and all her court were to set sail. Pale and sad, Constance prepared to go, since she knew

Everyone wept to see her go, but there was no help for it, and she was brought to the ship with all due ceremonies. "Farewell, fair Constance!" cried the people on shore who had come to see her off; and soon the bright sails faded from their sight.

Meanwhile, the sultana, the sultan's wicked old mother, saw that her son's taking a foreign bride and becoming a convert to another religion might be a fine opportunity for her to seize the royal power. She determined to try to turn the court against her son in hopes that he might be overthrown, so that she could rule the land herself.

The sultana therefore called her personal councilors around her for a secret conference, and said to them, "My lords, as you all know, my son is determined to give up the holy laws of the Koran, given to us by the prophet Mohammed—but I swear that I shall die before I let Mohammed's law pass from my heart! I assure you that we have nothing to gain by making ourselves slaves to this new law, and I fear God will punish us for turning away from our religion. Will you allow a foreign princess and a foreign law to overturn the ancient customs of our land, or will you stand with me? If you will promise to obey my wishes, I can save us from this tyranny."

By making such a pretense of doing it all for the sake of her religion, she soon persuaded her people, who swore to stand by her come what might. Then she told them her plan: "First, we shall all pretend to become Christians. Then, I shall give a feast in honor of the sultan's bride, and it shall be such a feast as shall quite take care of the sultan forever. He shall certainly never have need of food again, nor shall all the baptismal water in the world be able to wash away the blood in which his bride shall be bathed."

she must. No wonder, though, that she wept —for she was to be sent to a strange land to marry a man she had never seen and knew nothing about. "Farewell, my dear father and sweet mother," she said. "Remember your wretched daughter Constance. I must go to Syria, and perhaps I shall never see you again. I know it is my duty to go wherever you wish me to, and I shall always try to do whatever is right and proper."

This evil plan was accepted by her council, who swore secrecy and went on their way. The wicked sultana went to her son, and told him she was sorry she had been a heathen so long, and that she was anxious to become a Christian, too. She spoke many soft and flattering words, and deceived him so successfully that he was well pleased and kissed his mother with a glad heart.

When Constance and her party arrived in Syria, the sultan sent word to all the nobles of the land, particularly to his mother, that his bride had arrived, and he summoned them all to the wedding feast. A great crowd of richly dressed Syrians, led by the old sultana, went forth to meet the Romans. The sultana greeted her new daughter-in-law with a great show of gladness and affection. They all rode on to the palace for the royal wedding, where the sultan received them in a manner suitable to their rank and to the solemn occasion, and a splendid feast was held.

But when the feast was ending, their merriment also came to an end, for the old sultana gave a signal to her men. Suddenly they drew their knives and fell upon the guests, killing the sultan and every other Christian there excepting Constance. Not a single one of the Syrians who had been followers of the sultan was left alive. Then they took Constance and put her in a rudderless ship all by herself, and cast her out to sea, saying that if she could learn to sail she should return to Italy. As they well knew, the most skilled sailor in the world could not have steered a ship without a rudder! Yet they let her take some of her treasure, along with a good supply of food and clothing, and with these things in the boat she soon found herself drifting over the sea.

For many months poor Constance floated over the seas, expecting to drown at any moment, tossed by the wild waves and battered by the ocean winds. Three years and more passed, but somehow she managed to make her supply of food last. Finally, the waves cast her boat up on the shores of northern England, which was then a very wild and uncivilized country. But there was a castle where her ship had landed, and soon the steward of the castle, who was in charge in the absence of the king, came down to the beach to look at the wreck. He inspected

every part of the ship, and below the deck he found Constance, along with all her treasure. She was on her knees praying.

When she saw this strange man, the steward, she feared that he would kill her, and asked only that he kill her quickly, and end her misery. She asked this in her own native language, of course, which was a sort of Latin. The English steward understood her anyway, and felt very sorry for her. He brought the woeful woman gently to the shore, assuring her that she was safe.

Constance was thankful for her deliverance, but she made up her mind to tell no one who she was. Therefore she told the people, when they asked where she had come from, that she had been so dazed by her long, lone voyage that her mind was not quite clear, and that she really did not remember anything at all.

The steward and his wife, whose name was Hermengild, took such great pity on her that they could not help weeping over her. They took her back with them to their own home, where she lived happily for some time. Constance did all she could to help and please everyone around her, so that it was not long before all who knew her loved her as dearly as she had been loved by her own people back in Rome. The steward and his wife became particularly devoted to her, and all three lived together happily.

Unfortunately for Constance, however, her beauty and sweetness could not be expected to go unnoticed, and it soon happened that a young knight of the country fell in love with her, and courted her ardently. Constance did not trust this knight, for she felt that he was not an honorable man, and she therefore refused to listen to him. When she continued to refuse him, he became so angry that he determined to take revenge, and all his love turned to bitter hate.

One night, when the steward was away, the knight crept quietly into the steward's house, into the chamber where Dame Hermengild and Constance were sleeping. He went directly to Hermengild's bed and cut her throat; then he laid the bloody knife down beside Constance and quickly left.

deed, but the false knight appeared at the court and spoke against her, accusing her of the murder.

Everyone was grieved and astonished at this, and the people said among themselves that it did not seem possible that Constance, who had always been so good in every way, could have killed Dame Hermengild. Everyone knew how the two women had loved each other. Many stepped forward in the court and spoke in her defense, and all were in agreement that she could not have done it, except the real murderer, who continued to insist that Constance was guilty. This began to look rather suspicious to King Alla, and he asked more and more questions, trying to find out what the truth of the matter really was.

As Constance dropped down to her knees and prayed to be rescued from this false suspicion, the king looked at her pale face and felt tears of sympathy come to his eyes. "Go quickly and fetch the book," said he to one of the officials present, "and let us see if this knight will solemnly swear that she killed this woman."

They fetched a copy of the Bible, and the knight laid his hand upon it and swore that Constance was guilty. But the moment the words left his mouth an invisible hand hit him on the back of the neck, and he fell down dazed in full view of all the people gathered there, and blood poured from his mouth. A voice like the thunder was heard saying, "You have foully slandered an innocent—and shall I hold my peace?"

The people were dumfounded by this marvel, and all stood still as stones for several minutes. King Alla finally broke the silence, with a sharp command that the knight be taken and put to death. Alla then turned to Constance, raised her gently from the floor where she knelt, and asked her if she would be his wife.

During the night the steward returned and found his wife dead in her bed, and the knife lying where the knight had left it. What could Constance say? Horror and sorrow drove her nearly out of her wits, so that she could hardly speak to defend herself against the accusation of having killed Hermengild.

The steward went at once and told his king, whose name was Alla, all about this crime, and also all he knew about Constance —namely, that she had been found in a boat on their shore. The king called her to appear before him, and was moved with wonder and pity when he saw her. It seemed hard to believe that she could have done such a foul

Thus Constance became a queen, and the people of the land rejoiced greatly at her marriage to King Alla. But there was one person who was not at all happy about the royal wedding. The king's mother, Done-gild, a creature full of spite and hatred, thought it a terrible thing that her son should marry a foreigner and a stranger— a woman of whose family and earlier life nothing was known. The king, however,

paid no attention to her disapproval, and was happy with his lovely bride.

Some time later, King Alla had to make a journey to Scotland, but his wife could not go with him because she was expecting their first child. He therefore left Constance in the care of the steward and departed. While the king was away, she gave birth to a fine baby boy, whom she named Maurice. At once the steward summoned a messenger, giving him a letter to take to King Alla, with the happy news that he had a fine son. The messenger took the letter and set forth. But then he thought that it might be a good idea to pay his respects to the king's mother, too, so he went first to Donegild, and said, "Madame, I bring you good news: The queen has a boy child, to the great joy of the whole land. Look, I am carrying a letter to the king, telling him this happy news, and I must take it to him in all haste. If you would like to send along any messages of your own to your son, the king, I should be glad to carry them."

Donegild answered, "I have nothing to send him right now, but if you will spend the night here perhaps I shall have something to send along in the morning."

She had her servants give the messenger much ale and wine, so that he soon was sound asleep. One of them then stole his letter from him, and substituted another letter, a forgery, which Donegild had signed with the steward's name. This second letter said that Queen Constance had given birth to so horrible a monster that everyone in the castle was frightened out of his wits. The letter went on to say that they all thought Constance was a wicked fairy of some kind, and all men shunned her company.

The sorrow of King Alla when he received this letter was almost unbearable. Nevertheless, he did not speak of it to anyone, but sat down and wrote a letter back

to the steward saying, "God's will be done. Take good care of this child, be it foul or fair, along with my dear wife until I come home. Perhaps at some future date we shall be able to have a more agreeable heir."

Almost in tears, he sealed the letter and gave it to the messenger, telling him to be on his way at once.

But the careless and foolish messenger repeated what he had done before. Instead of going straight to the steward, he went first to the court of the king's mother. There he was again welcomed and entertained with such feasting and wine that he slept so soundly that Donegild was able once more to steal away his letter and substitute one which read: "The king commands his steward on pain of death not to allow Constance to remain in the country for more than three days. She shall be placed in the same ship in which she arrived, and her young son with her. They shall be pushed out to sea, with strict orders that they are never to return."

In the morning the messenger made his way to the steward, and gave him what he supposed was the king's letter. When the steward read the letter his hand shook and his grief was such that he wailed aloud, crying, "Alas, how can this be? Can it be true that the innocent should be so wickedly punished? Oh good Constance, woe is me for it seems that I must be your tormentor, or die myself!"

All the folk of the castle, young and old, were shocked and horrified, and there was constant mourning during the three days after the letter arrived. On the fourth day Constance came forth with a deadly pale face, carrying her baby son to the ship. She rocked the weeping child in her arms and said to him, "Peace, little son—I will not hurt you." Taking her kerchief from her own head, she covered his head with it; then, kneeling down before the steward, she said in her grief, "Poor little child, what is your guilt? Why does your stern father wish to destroy you? Have mercy, dear steward—let my little child stay here and dwell with you!"

The steward shook his head, unable to speak for sorrow, and Constance went on, "Then kiss him once, for his father's sake." She looked about her at the land where she had been queen. Then she rose, saying, "Farewell, ruthless husband," and walked down the beach to the ship, with all the people following her mournfully.

The ship was provided with a large amount of food and with everything else that was necessary for a long voyage on the open sea. Once more, Constance was set adrift and floated out to sea.

Soon afterwards the king came home to his castle and asked at once for his wife and child. At this, the steward felt a cold chill at his heart, and told the king exactly what had happened. He showed him the letter with its royal seal, saying, "Lord, you commanded me to do this on pain of death, and I have followed your orders." The messenger was summoned, and questioned until he admitted where he had spent the nights on his journey. At last the whole truth came to light. The king lost no time in arresting Donegild, who was condemned to death.

Alla lived in sorrow night and day, mourning for his wife and child. His grief was indescribable. Meanwhile Constance floated on the sea for more than five years before her ship finally approached land. This was near a castle in a strange country, and the people from the castle came and gazed in wonder at the ship. But during the night, the steward of the castle, who was quite a different sort of man from the steward of King Alla, came sneaking down to the ship, bent on carrying away Constance and her child into slavery and taking the ship's treasure for himself. Constance cried out for help, but there was no one near but her child, who could only weep. Somehow, though, she found the strength to struggle with this wicked man, so that by chance he lost his balance and fell overboard, and was immediately drowned.

In this manner Constance and her child were saved, but after so brutal an attack on her, she was naturally afraid to stay in that land. She pushed off from shore, and once again floated on the high seas. For many a weary day she floated, sometimes heading west and sometimes east, sometimes north and sometimes south, with never a sight of land or the homes of men.

In the meantime the emperor in Rome had received word of what had happened in Syria, and how all the Christian folk had been killed and his dear daughter dishonored and cast out. As soon as he had heard these tidings, the emperor sent an army to Syria to take vengeance, and after a long campaign his army completely wiped out the forces of the wicked sultana. After the successful conclusion of the campaign, the Romans established a governor to rule over Syria, and set sail for Rome again.

On the voyage back it happened that they met the ship in which sat Constance and her child. The senator who was general of the

Roman army inquired who she was, and how she came there, but she would not say. He had no idea who she might be, and in the end he took her home with him and turned her over to his wife, who welcomed Constance and her son to her household, even though none knew them. There they lived in peace and quiet for many years. The senator's wife was Constance's own aunt, but she did not recognize Constance after all these years, and Constance herself never breathed a word to let her know.

Back in England, King Alla, who had been weeping for his lost wife and child all these years, was also very unhappy that he had been forced to be the cause of his own

mother's death. In sorrow and repentance he decided to go to Rome and ask pardon of the pope.

Word quickly spread all over Rome that King Alla was coming on a pilgrimage, and the senator with whom Constance lived was appointed to go forth to meet him and to entertain him. It happened that Constance's son was in his party. Perhaps his mother had asked that he be taken, but in any case he was there at the feast, and in the course of it he did as his mother had told him, and went and looked carefully at Alla's face. The king was mystified by the boy, and asked his host, "Who is this child?"

"I have no idea who he is," answered the senator. "He has a mother, but no father that I know of." He went on to tell Alla how he had found the mother and child, and praised the mother as the most virtuous woman he had ever heard of.

The young boy looked as much like Constance as any creature could, and King Alla remembered well the face of his wife. He fell to wondering whether the child's mother could be his Constance, but finally he sighed, and scolded himself for being foolish, for he knew that his wife was probably dead long ago and at the bottom of the sea. Still, it seemed barely possible that there might be some hope of her having been saved again, as she had been before.

King Alla therefore went home with the senator, hoping against hope. The senator was highly honored to have such a guest in his home, and he sent at once for Constance, at Alla's request. I can scarcely say that Constance danced for joy at this—indeed, she could hardly stand on her feet when she was called. But she came and stood before the king, who was almost overcome with emotion, for he recognized her the minute he saw her. In her sorrow she stood silent as a statue, her heart heavy with distress as she remembered his unkindness. Twice she fainted away, and he wept and said, "Dear wife, I swear to you that I am not guilty of hurting you and my son, Maurice, who looks so like you," and he explained what had happened.

When Constance understood the truth they kissed a hundred times, and there was great joy between them. Some time later she asked her husband if he would invite her father, the Roman emperor, to dine with them, but she also begged Alla not to say a word about her to her father. He agreed, and the invitation was sent and accepted.

On the next day Alla and his wife rode forth to meet the emperor, Constance's father, in joy and happiness. When Constance saw her father coming towards her, she jumped down from her horse and knelt at his feet. "Father," said she, "I expect that you have quite forgotten your young child Constance. I am your daughter, whom you sent to Syria many years ago. I am she who was cast adrift on the wild seas in a rudderless boat. Have mercy on me now, good father, and do not send me off again, but thank my dear lord here for his kindness to me."

Who could have been happier than the members of this family, reunited at last, when none had thought ever to see each other again? In great joy and merriment they went on to dinner, where the senator and his wife joined in their happiness.

When the time came, King Alla took his sweet wife back to England, and there they lived happily a while until Alla's death.

After that Constance returned to Rome and lived a quiet life as a widow in her father's house, beloved by all as she had been in her girlhood. Her son Maurice was proclaimed heir to the Roman throne, and in later years he became emperor himself.

Thus they all lived to the end of their lives in peace and happiness. Now fare you well; my tale is at an end. May God send us all joy after woe, and bless all this good company.

*Here Ends the Man of Law's Tale*

*Chaucer never finished all the tales that were promised at the beginning. Neither did he tell how the pilgrims finished their journey, nor do we know which of them won the prize and the dinner that was to be awarded to the teller of the best tale—for Chaucer died before his book was finished.*

*The choice of the best tale-teller is really up to you. If you can make up your mind, eat your next good dinner in honor of him and of Geoffrey Chaucer, dead these five centuries and more. May he rest in peace.*